# WAKING OISIN

*Grace Kilian Delaney*

This book is dedicated to the people of Las Vegas who were affected
by the massacre in October of 2017. #Vegasstrong

# Acknowledgements

I'd like to thank my beta readers, Kim over at Kimmer's Book Banter, Roe, Silvia, and Matt, my editor at NineStar Press, Elizabetta, and to everyone who gave Oisin and Trent a chance—a special thank you! Your time and support are invaluable.

Oisin loves animals, and if you do too, please donate to your local shelter or volunteer. If you need financial aid for vet bills, visit Bestfriends.com for a list of companies in your state. Oisin thanks you and so does his fur baby, Maggie.

# Chapter One

OISIN HARRISON

As I walked out of my last class of the day, the wretched feeling grew larger in my stomach, and if it weren't for the cool January air, I might have puked. I'd failed my first project. My second semester at UNLV's law school was not going well, and I'd be lucky if I made it through the next four months without getting kicked out.

My father had been disappointed with my decision to attend our home state's college. Being the senior partner and founder of the most prestigious entertainment law firm, with locations in Las Vegas and Los Angeles, he'd had ridiculously high expectations for his youngest son. When he came home from LA on Friday, like he did every weekend, the news of my being on academic probation would be reported to him by one of his many acquaintances (aka babysitters) before I had an opportunity to plead my side, and a butt chewing would ensue.

I trudged back to my apartment where I found my best friend, Devon Thomson, in the parking lot getting out of his car. His makeup and short brown hair were flawless, and the stylish wrap coat he wore stopped just above his knees, leaving his calves exposed. The ease with which he expressed his femininity had always impressed me.

Devon picked up on my body language immediately. "You don't look too happy."

"I failed." My chest tightened. I'd never failed at anything before. I'd survived an undergrad degree in Biological Sciences and graduated summa cum laude, but I had no heart for law. Lately, I had no heart for anything; I was a zombie masquerading among the living.

Devon hugged me. "It's okay, Os. You'll do better next time—you always do."

That's why I loved my friend. He was always a hundred and ten percent supportive and affectionate. I missed our nights making love to each other as FWB and hanging out with him like we used to before he met his boyfriend. Whenever he talked about his lover, he glowed with happiness. I'd never seen him so happy, so in love, and it made any nostalgic desires I had seem trivial.

He released me and a wicked grin spread across his lips. "I got something that might cheer you up."

"I know that look, and it means trouble." I laughed, and it seemed like it'd been an eternity since that sound had come from me. "I'm in."

He clapped, his suede gloves dampening the sound. "We got invited to a record release party in Los Angeles next weekend, and I was thinking we could dress up like we used to? It's been too long since we had some fun together."

My heart swelled. Seemed I wasn't the only one missing our together time. I should stay and study. Be a good little student. But what Devon offered was too tempting. Screw it. I was going to LA. "Sounds perfect."

"Yay! I've got the best outfit for you. You're gonna look so hot, you'll be swatting off guys and girls."

"I don't know about that." Sometimes I thought being bisexual was a blessing, other times a curse. The curse had happened last semester when my fiancée determined my bisexuality was a cover for being gay and that one day I'd leave her for a man. I protested. She left anyway.

"I do," Devon affirmed, hooking his arm with mine and resting his head on my shoulder as we walked the few steps to my front door

"Who are you? Susie Sunshine?" I envied the confidence he had; it drew people to him. I couldn't remember the last time I felt safe or confident in my own skin.

He brought his hands to his face, framing it like a sun's rays. "Oh, you know me. Just a ray of light wherever I go."

"Will Stone be there?" Mentioning his boyfriend's name brightened his smile to megawatt proportions. I'd need sunglasses if he kept it up.

"Yep. And before you even ask—no, Matty will not be there."

Matty. Stone's bandmate, who'd brought me to his hotel room, kissed me, and then shoved me away. Last time I saw him, he apologized for leading me on. Alcohol made any hole look good until a hiccup of sobriety hit. Whatever. Matty had been my last attempt at getting laid, and that was so many months ago, I'd reinstated my virginity.

I let out a breath. "It won't matter if he's there, Dev. We're good. He's over it. I'm over it. It's not like he's the first person to reject me." That sounded more pathetic than I'd intended. Time to change the topic. "Do you mind if we stop by Paws for Love before getting dinner? There's someone I want to check in on."

"Wouldn't be one of those gorgeous redheaded veterinarians, would it?" Dev raised his perfectly arched eyebrows.

"Despite my crush on the twins, no. It's a female of the four-legged variety—much too hairy. I found a dog, a black lab, with a damaged leg."

Devon brushed my cheek with his gloved fingers. "You're so sweet, you know that?"

The familiar touch set up an ache in my heart, but not because I wanted to be in a relationship with him. Devon and I had been there, done that, and decided we were better off friends.

"Being sweet has done nothing for me."

"Ooh, you could get yourself a leather daddy, go all whips and chains. You know, be bad." Devon tapped a finger against his lips, his gaze shifted upward in thought.

"Seriously?" I struggled with the lock to the lemon-yellow front door, fighting back the disturbing image.

Devon lightly pushed me out of the way and turned the key twice before it gave. He plopped the key into my hand without acknowledging his triumph over the stubborn lock. "Might loosen you up some."

"Getting laid would loosen me up, never mind getting a leather daddy." I shouldered the door and went inside.

"I think we've found a goal for our LA trip." He rubbed his hands together.

I barked a laugh. "My dad always says it's good to have goals."

DEVON WAITED IN the car and called his boyfriend while I went to check on my girl. A few extremely nervous four-legged patients were in the veterinarian's waiting room. A fluffy, white Pomeranian shivered so hard I thought she might pee on her owner's lap, while the other two, some type of shepherd mix, whined and panted in anticipation.

For six years, I'd volunteered at Paws for Love, cleaning cages, mopping floors, and doing whatever tasks the owners would let me just so I could be closer to the career I wanted, rather than the one I felt bound to by blood ties.

"Oisin." Meredith Martin, a lithe redhead, and co-owner of the clinic greeted me. She and her identical twin were ten, maybe fifteen, years older than me, curvy, gorgeous, and happily married, and unfortunately so my type—minus the married part.

"Dr. Martin," I said, mocking formality and earning a smile.

"We didn't have any luck with Maggie's microchip, but we're still checking around to see if anyone is looking for her. Your girl is a strong one and is doing well. Go on back. Melissa will fill you in. I've got another patient." She pointed to the quaking white fur ball.

Maggie, as I named her since she had no ID, had been limping and tearing through an old fast food wrapper when I'd spotted her. I gained her trust by offering my lunch—a peanut butter and jelly sandwich, the only thing I knew how to make. That'd been enough to become best of friends, and I was able to get the emaciated animal into my car and to the clinic without any problems. She was too docile and trained to be a stray, but without a registered microchip, finding her pet parents would be difficult.

"I gave her fluids and reset her leg," Dr. Melissa Parker, Meredith's twin, said after exchanging hellos.

"What about the mass?" During her initial exam, Melissa had found a lump in the dog's uterus and X-rayed it. "Are you going to do a biopsy?"

"I'll do it after I remove the mass to determine whether it's cancerous or not. It's pressing on her bladder, and she's probably in pain." Melissa sat at a counter filled with computers and lab equipment. "We'll have her blood work back on Monday and then we can make whatever decision we need to, okay?"

I nodded, understanding the darker meaning behind Melissa's words. If there was an issue with the dog's blood work, then an operation might not be doable. If that were the case, it'd be kinder to send the old girl home with nothing but painkillers.

"Will you be taking her?"

"My apartment won't let me have a dog, and I doubt my mom wants another furry in the family."

"I'll tell you what, if we don't find her owners, she can stay with me until you find a way to keep her."

"Thank you. How much do I owe you? And please don't argue with me." Paying for Maggie's care was one of the few things in my life I could control.

"Oisin," she protested. "Keep your money, or if you really want to pay, donate the fees to the Pet Parent Assistance Fund."

"You're amazing. I'd kiss you if your husband wouldn't get jealous."

"I might take that kiss anyway. It'll make Gareth appreciate what he's got when he sees a younger man fawning over me." Melissa winked.

"Please, that man worships you." The times I'd seen them together, there was nothing but love in his eyes. They even had a sweet daughter, Nina, whom I'd occasionally colored with when they brought her to work.

"And what about you? Any luck in the dating department?"

"Let's just say Death Valley has seen more rain than I've seen action."

"My brother's visiting from out of town. Let me set the two of you up."

"I appreciate the thought, but I think it's best if I focus on school."

"You're young. You should be out there getting some."

"Says the woman who met her husband as an undergrad."

"True. But you can't let what happened with Carrie destroy your love life forever. You're too smart and too good-looking to live the life of a monk."

I cringed. I never said her name and hated hearing it.

"I'll tell you what. I'll ask my brother anyway, okay? I think you'll get along."

"Do I get to see a picture of him before you set me up? He could be a troll."

"Not with these genes." She brought her hand to her chest. "How dare you insult my family!"

"As long as he has all his teeth and hair, I guess I've got nothing to lose. Sure. Go for it."

"All hair and teeth accounted for last time I saw him." She grinned. "Oh! I can't believe I almost forgot to tell you. I got ahold of Mr. Wheeler, the head of veterinary medicine at UC Davis. He said your application and essay looked good and to go ahead and submit them."

"Really? That's... Wow...oh God." I worried my lip, sucking on my piercing. It'd been a dream, and this was like a winning lottery ticket. "I can't believe you did that for me. Thank you."

"It's my alma mater. I got the hookup. Besides, you belong working with animals, not in some law office."

I swallowed around the lump in my throat. "You're completely—"

"Yeah, I know. I'm amazing." Melissa tossed her red hair in an overdramatic gesture, something Devon would do if he had long hair.

"You are." I hugged her.

"I think you've kept Maggie waiting long enough, and I've got to get back to work."

"Slacker."

"You know it!" She lifted her chin, looking smug. "Your pup was sleeping last time I checked on her. She'll be happy to see you."

I walked past the exam rooms and into the heart of the animal hospital where a couple cats and dogs rested in cages. Maggie was in a bottom cage. An unyielding cast prevented her from standing with any grace. When she saw me, her stocky tail thudded happily as she struggled to stand. We hadn't spent more than a few hours together before I brought her to the clinic, but I swear she remembered me.

"Hey, girl." I squatted and stuck my fingers through the bars to scratch her head and neck. "It's okay. You don't have to get up. Lie down." I pointed to the ground, and when she did as I asked, I resumed petting her. "We'll get you a good home, maybe even with me." She gave an approving wag of her tail before drifting off to sleep.

I'd always heard if you loved what you did, then it didn't feel like work. That was how I felt while getting my bachelor's degree. The courses had been rigorous, but I loved it. It'd opened the possibility of combining my love for animals with my passion for science. Carrie's dad had been ill on and off my senior year of college, and she'd wanted to stay close to him. As in a ten- to twenty-minute car ride close. Moving to another city to study veterinary medicine, never mind California where I really wanted to go, had not been an option. I understood and figured as long as we were together, I'd be happy. And I was. Sort of. Not really.

Melissa had pushed me to apply. "Just try and see, Os. There's no harm in exploring your options, right?"

Right. And now it was an option.

"Should I go to California?" I asked a snoring Maggie. Without the financial support of my father and my monthly stipend from the trust, both of which I had no doubt would be severed should I approach my father with this drastic career change, I wouldn't be able to afford veterinary school. That's what had happened to my brother when he went for a performing arts degree from NYU instead of Stanford Law. I wasn't sure how he'd managed to pay for college but suspected his husband or his husband's family had helped out. If he hadn't been overseas working on a play, I'd ask him.

Even if I had the resolve to approach my father, he wouldn't listen. Something had changed between us over the past two years. There'd been no defining moment, more like a slow-growing discord that worsened each time we spoke. Growing up, I could pretty much tell him anything, but now our communication revolved around law classes and grades. If I deviated, he'd shut down, making it impossible to speak with him. So I'd given up trying. I missed the dad who used to play basketball and catch, the dad I could just hang out with, the dad I used to aspire to be like, the dad I could tell anything to and not worry about his disapproval. The current version of my father was impenetrable.

I scratched the sleeping dog's neck. "I'll find a way to keep you." Maybe someday I'd stand up to my father, but not now. I was going to have dinner with my friend and get so drunk I'd forget everything. I gave Maggie a final pat and left.

# Chapter Two

OISIN

Hollywood was full of heat, smog, and strange inhabitants—all on par with the Vegas Strip—and navigating through the Hollywood Hills with all its narrow streets and ups and downs was nauseating. I was grateful Stone had a driver pick us up at the airport. All the houses were crammed together and smaller than my childhood home on the outskirts of Vegas, and the streets were barely wide enough to let a single car through. When Devon and I finally pulled into the driveway of Stone's Spanish-style mansion, I'd expected something bigger and more decadent from the tattooed rock star than the well-manicured property.

We'd been buzzed in at the gate so it wasn't surprising to find the rocker standing in front of the house. The driver hadn't even put the car in park when Devon jumped out and launched himself into Stone's arms, showering him with kisses.

"I think he missed you," I said as I approached. I might as well have been talking to the fountain out front. My best friend clung on to his lover like a hundred-fifty-pound marmoset monkey and sucked Stone's face like he possessed the only oxygen on the planet.

Instead of gawking like a creeper, I got my carry-on bag and Devon's two giant suitcases—because the man thought a two-day trip required packing half his closet—and waited until the suck fest was over.

"I missed you, babe," Stone panted, smoothing the back of Devon's head and gazing at him with hearts in his eyes. If the weekend was going to be this disgustingly lovey-dovey, I might have to find another place to stay. Hopefully, Stone had a separate wing somewhere in that house of his so I wouldn't have to listen to them humping each other into kingdom come.

"I missed you too."

"Hi there. Remember me? Your audience?" I waved.

"Os. What's up, man?" Stone casually returned my gesture as if he hadn't nearly boned my BFF in front of me. He adjusted himself and led us into his home.

I expected the place to have a Gothic vibe, or maybe have Harley Davison motorcycles hanging out, pool table, bar—things that screamed a badass rock star lived here. Aside from the platinum records lining the stairwell to the second floor, the décor was inviting and cozy. I could totally crash on that comfy sectional he had in the living room and chill in front of the fifty-two-inch TV hanging above the fireplace.

"I can't stay long," Stone said. "I have an interview, and then I have to get to sound check."

"But we just got here," Devon whined and clasped his boyfriend's hand, bringing it to his crotch.

"Um, I'll just go outside and let you guys...do...each other." I plopped our bags down in the middle of the living room, since Stone and Devon were already immersed in tongues and touches, and headed through the pristine kitchen and into the backyard, where a small succulent garden resided.

Less than thirty minutes later, they resurfaced wearing matching postorgasmic glows.

"I'll see you later, beautiful." Stone kissed Devon's hand.

"Bye, sexy," I said, because I was in a mood. Stone laughed and waved goodbye.

"Better?" I said, as we sat at the kitchen table that, judging by the look of it, was once a giant wood door.

"Much."

I shook my head.

We ordered food and ate before getting ready for the show. Devon had big plans for our makeup and outfits and said the "artiste" needed time to create his masterpieces—us in drag.

He lugged his suitcases up to Stone's massive bedroom on the second floor, and I trailed behind him.

"He's got this amazing bathroom with perfect lighting." Devon motioned as we went deeper into the spacious room. This area, unlike the rest of the house, was lived in. There were clothes strewn across the bed, multiple pairs of shoes and boots scattered by the walk-in closet, and an overflowing laundry basket by the bathroom. Stone's closet contents rivaled those of my best friend's. If they ever moved in together, they'd need an extra bedroom to fit their combined wardrobes.

Devon rubbed his hands together. "All right, let's get to work!"

After two hours of fussing, primping, and preening, and goofing off, Devon finished.

"You look amazing, Os," he said, appraising his mad makeup skills. We were in high school when Devon began cross-dressing in public. The first time he did it, I joined him to show support. He was afraid people would mock him, and justifiably so, but he wanted to be true to himself and wear what he felt comfortable in. Our onetime thing then turned into Girls Night Out where a couple times a month we'd dress up and go club-hopping, something we'd continued until last year when I'd gotten engaged. It made my fiancée uncomfortable, so I didn't do it often. I missed it, though. I liked the makeup, the panties. Especially the panties. I secretly wore them under my day clothes from time to time.

"Okay, you can look now." Devon spun me around so I faced the vanity mirror.

The person staring back at me was stunning and feminine, almost unrecognizable. Devon had contoured my face, bringing out my cheekbones, and slimming my nose. It also made my hazel eyes—altered by brown contacts—pop.

"Dev, I look—"

"Absolutely beautiful. I know. I'm a genius." He huffed on his long nails and then polished them on his shirt. "I've been watching a lot of YouTube, and there's some seriously brilliant makeup tips on it. I'm so happy you're doing this, Os. I've completely missed our Girls Nights Out. Now, let's get you dressed."

I stripped out of all my clothing—I'd been naked with Devon too many times for it to matter—and stared at the gaff he held out to me. "I'm not wearing that."

"Don't even want to try?"

"I've no desire to push my balls up, sorry. What happened to the bra and tight panties?"

"Got those too." He went into his suitcase and pulled out a pair of underwear with a tag on it and a black basque with clamps on the bottom for stockings. I got excited about wearing the basque, even if it meant my waist would be squished. He shuffled through more clothing and found a black bra-like thing that squeezed my chest together for the illusion of breasts. Devon helped me with everything except the stockings, which I managed on my own, finally fastening them to the basque.

"Ooh la la. You look hot. But just one more thing…" He handed me prosthetic breasts. "They're inserts."

I once felt a girl up who had implants. These felt like a close second. "I think I'll pass. I kinda like the way this thing looks without the fake boobs."

"Okay. You won't really need them with the outfit anyway." He put them back without protest. "So I thought a black-and-metallic dress would be the best thing for you to wear tonight." He held up the dress—the incredibly short dress—with its puffy skirt that would hide my junk. "Damn, you're gonna look so hot in this." He wolf whistled as he handed it to me. I put it on and was surprised when, combined with the basque, it gave me an hourglass shape. "Now the wig." He pinned my hair up and secured the black long-haired wig. Darn thing was itchy.

After Devon finished fussing with my hair and outfit, I stood in front of the full-length mirror in awe. The look was super sexy in a dirty-Goth way, even if not one body part was comfortable in the outfit. Oisin Harrison, mild-mannered law student, had morphed into a Goth princess. I'd never pass as a woman, not like Devon. My friend was seriously beautiful, like supermodel status. He had the height, the long, graceful limbs, and the confidence to trot down catwalks with the best of them. But this lady in the reflection—she was pure sin. Sin…yeah. That's what I'd call myself. Sin.

"Dev, you outdid yourself this time."

I probably should've shaved my legs. Dark hair and tattoos showed through the black nylon stockings. And the panties weren't going to hide an erection, either. I barely fit in them, and something about that made me feel dirty and sexy… Yeah. I liked it.

He stood behind me and rested his hands on my shoulders. "Oh, girl, you look amazing. I'm a fashion genius."

"That you are." I put my hand on his as we stood looking at our reflections.

Devon moved away and picked up a tube of lipstick from his ginormous makeup case. He applied the ruby-red color, puckered, and blotted with a tissue.

"Perfect. All set?"

"Just need the boots, and we're ready to go." I put them on. Wondering if I could walk in the five-inch heels, I took a few tentative steps around the room. Not too bad. I stumbled and latched onto Devon's arm. Not too good either.

"You'll get the hang of it, don't worry."

I wished he sounded more convincing. "I hope so. Otherwise, I'm gonna twist an ankle." I steadied myself and tried walking some more.

"It's the hips, Os. Move them and keep your head level. Like this." Devon paraded around the room in his death-defying stilettos, swishing his hips right and left, elegant and graceful. "Your turn."

I wobbled for the first steps. After the fourth, I found a rhythm. Dev was right— working the hips helped. It also made me feel kinkier, more feminine, more fitting of this Goth persona. I smiled triumphantly when I made an entire loop around the bedroom without stumbling. "I got this," I declared, putting a hand on my hip for emphasis.

"Then it's showtime!" Devon clapped, beaming with excitement.

# Chapter Three

TRENTON FISHER

I stood in my Century City office staring out the window at the sprawling cityscape below, the thrum of success coursing through my blood. My client had just signed the multi-million dollar clothing endorsement contract I'd spent the past two months negotiating. The hefty deal practically guaranteed I'd be one step closer to attaining partnership (or at least junior partnership) status at Harrison, Preston, and Bryant, Inc., the elite LA entertainment law firm where I'd been working since graduating from Harvard Law.

"May I come in?"

Andrew Harrison, senior partner and founder of the firm, appeared in the doorway to my office. Harrison—no one called him by his first name—stopped by my office a couple times a week, something that began when he'd first hired me as a clerk straight out of grad school. We'd continued the routine as an informal way to catch up on cases. We seldom discussed personal matters, or at least his personal life. He'd occasionally ask about my mom and sisters, who all lived in Nevada, where another branch of the firm existed. But I preferred California and its fast-paced life.

"Yes, of course."

I'd seen the many moods of my boss. He was fair and diplomatic to work for, but a terror if you were the opposition. Throughout my years with the firm, he'd been a mentor and role model. And a man I'd never want to cross. Recently, he'd been more on edge, less like the diplomatic man I'd met years ago. Rumors had floated around the office about him having an affair and that his wife of nearly thirty years had found out. I'd rather not believe the worst of my boss. It was innocent until proven guilty, after all.

"Congratulations on the Nelson contract. That was an outstanding feat." The other thing about my boss—he always gave praise when earned.

"Thank you, sir."

"How many times do I have to tell you to call me Harrison? Everyone else does."

"Harrison."

"That's better." He sat in one of the black leather seats across from my desk. "I have a proposition, and if you do it and do it well, I'll send your name to the board for junior partnership consideration."

This was it. The break I needed. I mentally salivated. "What is it?"

"I need someone in my Vegas branch that I can depend on. An attorney is going on maternity leave, so you'd be filling in for her initially. After you've settled in, you'll be overseeing the two new hires I'm bringing on in May or June."

My stomach curled. I'd left Vegas and all my family years ago and never thought about returning. The city felt void of life—a wasteland of excess. I tried to persuade my family to move to California. They stayed put. I should've been happy I'd be living closer to them, not having this bile rising in the back of my throat. Vegas felt like a dead end, not a promotion.

My family would expect Sunday dinners and occasional visits. And then there was my matchmaking sister Melissa. She'd scrambled to find Mr. Right for me after seeing how depressed I was during my visit at Christmastime. For the first time in eight years, my boyfriend Nic and I didn't decorate the tree or exchange gifts with my family. He complained I never made time for him—that work was my priority, not our relationship—and broke up with me.

"Is this a permanent transfer?" The thought of leaving California gutted me. I loved living near the ocean. West Hollywood wasn't close to the beach, but definitely closer than Nevada. I should've made more time to go dip my feet in the water.

"A year, maybe longer if you do well. You'll maintain your key clients naturally, and you'll be required to come back to LA for networking. We'll have the firm set you up with a house—a nice one. Big backyard. Quiet neighbors. You'll have the best of both worlds, like I do. I'll give you until Monday to decide." He rose from the chair. "Have a good time tonight."

Harrison offered a golden ticket, and I'd be an idiot to refuse. The opportunity was exactly what I'd been striving toward. My answer was yes. It had to be. I could manage a few years there and return to California. *I think.*

I gathered my laptop and a handful of briefs to familiarize myself with over the weekend. The long day wasn't over. Mutant Militia, my client, had a performance later, and part of my livelihood depended on networking and social appearances. *No rest for the wicked.*

The band members were basically children, barely twenty-one, and their music style combined electronic with acoustic instrumentation. As performers, they had that "thing," that extra spark that made them stand out in the saturated music scene. I'd had a hand in their success from the beginning. Knowing that gave me a sense of accomplishment, and supporting them whenever and wherever I could was important to me.

It had been a good day. I deserved to celebrate, maybe get laid, and definitely be proud and happy. But neither emotion surfaced as I ate dinner, and they remained absent as I rode to the club. I thought about heading to the beach instead, to savor the time I had left in California. Good thing Georgia texted me, confirming she'd be at the club. Seeing my college friend would be the perfect antidote to my maudlin mood.

THE TROUBADOUR WAS packed, and the crowd continued to grow. I searched for Georgia and found her near the bar. Dressed in a red steampunk-inspired outfit, she was impossible to miss. I swear if I had any inclinations toward women, Georgia would be my type.

"Trenton Fisher," Georgia sang in her southern drawl as she gave me a big hug. "So good to see y'all again. It's been too long. How ya holding up, sugar?" She knew about Nic and me splitting. I'd spoken with her at a BDSM convention in LA six months ago—just days after Nic left. I'd been so angry. So betrayed. Georgia offered to let me Dom one of her newbie subs. I declined. That was something I did solely for Nic because I loved him.

"Busy as usual."

"Hmm." She studied me. "Nope, not buying it. Let's get a drink, and you can tell your Domme all about it." She patted my shoulder and flagged down the bartender. I had to laugh. Georgia's uncanny ability to read people, especially me, was amazing. I was good at it. It was part of what made me a fantastic negotiator, but she was practically a mind reader.

We'd met at Boston University my sophomore year, two years before I'd met Nic. She'd been a Domme back then, too, studying to get her doctorate in psychiatry. I liked kink on occasion, but Nic loved being a sub, something we discovered under Georgia's tutelage. The three of us bonded while exploring D/s dynamics. I'd sub for her, and she'd supervise as I switched roles to dominate Nic. When Nic left, so did my desire to be a Dom. The lifestyle had been his choice, not mine. I'd enjoyed it because he enjoyed it.

Having procured our drinks, we moved to a less crowded space in the club. The opening band had started and the loudness level made conversation difficult.

"Spill," Georgia yelled in my ear, a necessity as the bass and guitars drenched the room. She stared at me expectantly before taking a healthy pull from her beer.

I leaned closer and shouted, "My boss is sending me to Vegas. It's a step toward the partnership I want."

"Congrats." She clinked her plastic cup against mine—the club forbade glass. "So why do you look like someone's pissed on your pant leg?"

"Well, I—" My heart stopped beating when I saw Nic standing several feet behind Georgia with his muscular arm wrapped around some equally muscular god-like man. He'd moved on quickly, that bastard.

Georgia, after turning and seeing my ex, twined her arm in mine and led me away from them toward the other side of the club before the wonder twins could see me gaping. "What's he doing here, and who is that tramp he's with?" she growled like a protective lioness. "The nerve of that boy."

"Nic was there when I discovered Mutant Militia. He's a huge fan." I should've expected he'd be here. He knew as many people in the industry as I did. We used to share clients. Lawyers and personal trainers—two must-haves in the industry.

"Forget about him, sugar."

I tried. I tried to not think about Nic and the lazy college mornings we'd spent naked together as I quizzed him about anatomy for his kinesiology degree, the nights we'd spent grinding against each other making love, or the business and social events we'd attended. It was the little things that I missed the most. He'd have coffee ready for me in the morning, my shirts pressed, and I'd bring home food from his favorite vegan restaurant, rub his legs as we watched television. I missed him lying next to me as we slept. Six months, and I hadn't gotten used to sleeping alone.

The music stopped, and Nic and his new man exchanged hugs and handshakes with people I didn't recognize. My heart sank. He'd already made new friends in his new life. I had...my career goals.

"Looks like the other band's coming on," she said, nudging my elbow and pointing to the stage.

The emcee took the mic, welcoming the crowd and doing some promo spots while plugging the radio station where he worked. When finished, he made an unexpected announcement.

"All right you guys, we got a special treat for you. Put those hands together and give it up for Stone Manson!" The crowd screamed and hollered and booed when they saw Stone take the stage with a guitar strapped over his shoulder. A distorted chord rang out, and Mutant Militia jumped on their instruments, backing him. Once again, music and screaming fans filled the room.

I had no idea Stone would be here, though his support was welcome. Stone's Army was a well-known band with a decade worth of fans, some of whom were here judging by the sound of people singing along with him. His presence would give my clients an added boost of media attention.

Curiosity had me scoping the room, searching for his boyfriend. I'd seen pictures of the femme dark-blond man. Stone had broken up with his longtime girlfriend last year, and him now having a boyfriend was a shock to friends and fans alike. No one knew he was bi. I had to hand it to him for coming out so boldly once news of their relationship spread. He said if anyone had a problem with him being with a man, they could go fuck themselves.

"Want another?" Georgia lifted her empty cup.

"Yeah. I got it." I returned to the bar and waited.

The bartenders were working with lightning-fast speed, filling drinks, taking payments, and moving with a mastered precision. They seemed to have a second sense of knowing where each other were. Unlike the patrons. Someone pushed me, sending me tumbling toward the woman standing in front of me at the bar. A strong tattooed arm wrapped around my waist before I made contact, and the musculature of it was masculine despite the very womanly appearance of its owner.

"I'm so sorry!" she shouted in a voice deeper than I'd anticipated. "Are you okay?"

"I'm fine," I replied, steadying myself and getting a good look at her. Her heavy makeup was tastefully done, accentuating her expressive brown eyes and high cheekbones. A silver-and-black dress fit her waist snuggly and flared at her hips. She was a he for sure, a Goth with a small barbell in the middle of her bottom lip.

"I'm no good in heels." She raked the piercing behind her top teeth. The sight went straight to my groin. I was already imagining how the smooth metal would feel sliding along my shaft, how those blood-red lips would look around my cock. It'd been ages since I'd been this attracted to someone, and never someone in high heels and a dress.

"Let me buy you a drink," I offered.

"I should be offering you a drink since I nearly knocked you over." She licked her lips—hot *damn*—and gave me the sweetest coy smile. It was as innocent as a schoolgirl's. She probably was a schoolgirl, or a schoolboy, or maybe even nonbinary. I'd have to find out how she identified. Regardless, she was definitely much younger than me.

"I insist."

"Well, if you insist." She motioned for me to step up to the bar.

"Trent!" Fate was not my friend. I'd forgotten about Nic, and here he was, grabbing my arm and standing so close I could feel the heat emanating from his thick body. His approach caught me completely off guard, leaving me speechless. I'd been entirely captivated by the hot young piece of ass who'd bumped into me.

"This is Brian." Nic gestured to the guy next to him, who sized me up with a disapproving sneer.

I had to pull myself together. All the oxygen left the room, replaced with fire and rage. I wanted to hit Nic. Yell at him. Tell him he was a fucking asshole for not sticking by me—that I was going to make partner, and all he had to do was wait one year. That was it. One. Fucking. Year. The anger robbed me of my voice.

"I'm Nic," he said, extending his hand to the woman I'd just offered to buy a drink for.

"I'm Sin," she replied, accepting my former lover's meaty paw.

*And I'm fucked. Sin? Seriously? That's like a porn name. Is it short for Cindy? Sinclair?*

"How long have you two been going out?" Nic eyed us suspiciously. As if he had any right to ask or look at Sin with that judgmental stare.

"None of your fucking business. That's how long," I snapped. If I could have shot lasers out of my eyes at him, I would have. The fucking nerve of this guy! And to think I used to love him, and now he was brazenly waltzing over here, shoving his new boy toy in my face. I turned to his lover and said, "Does he scream, 'Daddy make me come' when you beat him into submission? He used to love it." Nic never did that. I was being a cock, and judging by the mortified look on Brian's face, I'd hit my mark.

"Ignore them, baby," Sin said as she walked her fingers up my chest and looked me dead in the eye, asking permission for something. I nodded, not sure what I was agreeing to and didn't fucking care as long as it meant Nic would be out of my sight.

I hadn't expected a kiss. And damn, she could kiss. She toyed with my lips one at a time, nipping and sucking each one before slanting her mouth across mine. One flick of her hot tongue across the seam unleashed a feverish need to possess her. I took charge, diving into her mouth, teeth and tongues clashing. The taste of her had me rock solid, eager to get inside that tight ass and fuck her until she was an incoherent, sated mess. Everyone in the club could've disappeared at that point, and I wouldn't have noticed. Sin's lips were my new heaven, and I could have spent the rest of the night sucking and fucking them.

The final brush of her lips against mine was a tenderness reserved for lovers, not strangers, leaving me off balance. She'd been doing me a favor, helping me get back at my former lover by making him jealous. The moan I'd felt during our exchange told me she didn't mind, but I'd let myself get out of control, and I hated being out of control.

Our eyes stayed locked as we separated. She kept her hand resting on my chest and her arm around my back, as if we'd held each other like this a million times before.

"Guess I'll see you around," Nic responded in a clipped tone.

"Guess so," I replied without looking away from the beauty in front of me.

Sin scanned the area, a grin on her lips. "Coast is clear." I braved a look, seeing the back of my ex and his new lover. Mission accomplished. I should've felt better about the whole thing. Or at least happy that I'd pissed him off, and he'd had to leave.

This stunt ruined my chances of getting Nic back...

Did I want him back? Not really. He'd expected so much of me. I'd had to maintain everything while he thought he could just be a cute little sub. It had been my job to please him, to dream up new and inventive ways of getting him off, extending his pleasure—all while making sure the bills were paid, things around the house were fixed, groceries were bought. Fucking everything. As my sub, I should've ordered him to do it. But I didn't ask for the role of full-time Dom and grew to resent Nic's needy sub routine. I liked the once or maybe twice a week kinky play we used to do. I wanted us to be equals in our relationship. The imbalance in our relationship, combined with work, nearly killed me. *Shit.* It may have been one of the reasons I worked such long hours.

*What a time to have an epiphany.*

There was a brief lull in the club noise as the emcee thanked Stone and Mutant Militia and announced T-shirt and concert ticket giveaways for the band.

"Hey, I'm sorry if I overstepped," Sin said and wiped my lip with her thumb, making me wonder if I'd drooled and not noticed. Her lipstick remained smudge free. "I hate it when ex's appear out of nowhere."

My arm rested at her hip. I was afraid of letting go—afraid of losing this stranger's connection. The contact anchored me: To this place. To this moment, as my past trudged forward, impeding my thoughts.

"What he did was a total douche canoe move. 'How long have you been dating?'" She mocked Nic's snarky tone. "My ex did the same thing to me, rubbing her new boyfriend in my face."

Her? A new horror flashed in my mind. A cross-dressing straight guy just kissed me with tongue so I could save face in front of my ex. That was a seriously crazy move. Arousing and disappointing, too.

"I'm bi," she said almost defensively, like she was testing my reaction. I must have unintentionally broadcasted my shock when she mentioned her ex. "And I'm usually not dressed so...feminine."

"I'm gay," I replied. And wasn't it odd to blatantly declare our sexual identity? But I was grateful she wasn't straight. "When you say you're 'usually not so feminine,' do you mean—"

"I'm a he, not a she. I wear a little guyliner here and there, but tonight's outfit is just for fun."

He. Him. Good to know.

The music and the screaming crowd grew considerably louder as the emcee announced Mutant Militia. The band immediately launched into their first song. White lights flashed around the room catching Sin's delicate face, making my head spin from the whirlwind of a day I was having.

I needed another drink.

"It was nice meeting you, Trent. I'm sorry if I caused trouble." His breath was warm on my neck, and it'd be sexy as hell if he didn't have to shout over the music. When he started to slide out of my arm, I panicked, unwilling to release him. I was drawn to him. No one had ever defended me the way he had.

I pulled Sin back so he could hear me—it had nothing to do with me wanting to be closer. "Hey, what about that drink?"

He bit back a smile and nodded.

The bar was less crowded as the majority of fans had moved to the stage area, making it easier to order. I bypassed getting a drink for myself to keep a hand on Sin. Two hands weren't enough.

"I have to give this to my friend." I handed Sin one of the two drinks. With my hand on his lower back, we made our way through the audience as the music died down and Mark, the singer, spoke to the crowd. Georgia saw the two of us approaching and waved us over.

"Well, well. Leave for a drink; bring back a beauty. Trent—so thoughtful. I'm Georgia, and you are gorgeous."

"Down, girl." A smidgen of unexpected jealousy rose. Georgia preferred women, but I knew she'd made exceptions in the past. Normally, I was eloquent. It's what made me good at my job—good at making deals and getting what I wanted, and I wanted Sin. I'd been too thrown by Nic's presence to maintain casual conversation. Georgia getting to do it before me annoyed me.

Sin bit his lip again and smiled bashfully at Georgia. "I'm Sin, and thank you. But I got nothing on you." He waved his hand demonstratively down my friend's rocking body.

"What brings you here? Fan, friend, industry?" Georgia sipped her drink.

"My friend invited me. He's with his boyfriend over there somewhere." Sin motioned with his beer.

I watched him scan the crowd, noting a pinch of tension around his eyes. I was transfixed as his tongue darted from his mouth, wetting his lips, taunting me to take another taste. When he caught me staring, the corners of his perfect mouth crept up in a smile.

Georgia and Sin continued talking—or shouting—but the music prevented me from understanding a single word. Sin laughed. Georgia laughed. Aggravation flowed through me along with irrational jealousy. My sole consolation was that Sin remained by my side with my hand still around his waist. I could feel the stiff fabric of the corset under his dress, the heat of his body penetrating it. Trying to picture what he looked like in just the corset made my cock twitch. Sin was not my usual type. Muscular, beefy, demigods who were versatile usually did it for me. There was nothing hotter than fucking a muscleman. The dichotomy of the person in my arms was new and something I'd never considered exploring.

Georgia gave me a sly grin and tucked her phone between her breasts. A handy little spot. My phone vibrated.

*I'm leaving you two alone. Got me a hot date with a sexy mama.*

Georgia wiggled her fingers in a farewell and sashayed toward the exit. The woman must have had a sixth sense because just then the band finished their last song. The boisterous crowd screamed and hollered, the cheering all muffled in my ears as if I'd stuffed cotton in them.

Sin reached into his purse and pulled out his phone, texted something and put it back. "My friend," he offered without further explanation.

"Do you—" The club lights came on, and I saw how young Sin appeared. Barely twenty, if I had to guess. I'd be thirty-one this year.

"Something wrong?" He took a breath and twisted his lips, disappointment clear upon his baby face.

"No...you're just...young." I thought about checking his ID.

"Old enough that you won't go to jail, if that's what you're worried about. How old are you? Thirty-five, forty?"

Jesus. Did I really look that old?

"Thirty," I grumbled.

"I like older guys," he amended apologetically.

Taking Sin to bed was a stupid idea, and not solely because of our age difference. I had entirely too much work—briefs to look over, contracts to review. I'd planned on doing it when I got home so I could take some of Saturday off. Fuck it. I had celebrating to do. The firm had rooms booked at the Roosevelt for the event, one of which I knew was under my name. Being with Sin would be the perfect way to celebrate my recent negotiation.

"Do you want to come back to my hotel for a drink?"

"A drink? Something tells me you want more than a drink. But yeah, I'd like that."

My pulse ticked up a few notches. "Let's go."

I LED US through the club and out the front door where the traffic on Santa Monica Boulevard crawled, making me grateful for the firm's foresight in booking a nearby hotel. I called the driver—a company perk for the evening—and told him to meet us by the entrance.

"Where are we going?" Without the cacophony of the club masking it, the true color of his tenor voice was pleasant, melodic, and laced with concern.

"The Roosevelt. Room 314. Is that all right? It's down the boulevard a little ways."

"Yes, that's fine. I just want to let my friend know." He texted the information and took my hand after he finished. Tension remained along his forehead and around his eyes.

Boldly, I cupped his face, smoothing my thumb along his cheek. It'd be no fun for either of us if he were uncomfortable. "I'll take care of you, baby. Don't worry. We don't have to do anything you don't want to do."

"I want this." He turned his head and kissed my palm. His lips were warm, the barbell on his bottom lip, hot and smooth.

The kiss triggered a hunger to taste and feel his lips on mine. I pulled him toward me, my hand at the base of his skull for leverage. Fiery greed consumed me, and I had to have him. He accepted without resistance, parting his lips, inviting me in. His body relaxed as our tongues met, and his flavor was pure intoxication, an equal blend of sweet and spicy from the beer he'd been drinking. He kissed delicately, more like a woman than a man, and I wondered if it was intentional. In the end, I'd make him lose that control; I'd ensure unbridled pleasure consumed every inch of his body.

The drive to the hotel, which was about four miles from the club, took an impossibly long thirty minutes. There was no privacy window in the town car, otherwise I'd have been kissing, touching, and stroking the beautiful man next to me.

"You must be someone important if you've got a car and are staying at the Roosevelt." He shifted nervously, switching the crossing of his legs and smoothing out his skirt.

The naïveté killed me. People put on airs all the time in this city. They'd rent pricey rooms, lease an expensive car, buy clothes they couldn't afford, all to create an illusion to appear more important than they were. Rising through the ranks, I'd seen my fair share of posers.

"I've worked hard for this luxury. Are you new to the Los Angeles area?"

"I'm just visiting. I'm from out of town, actually. But my dad commutes to LA. He's got a business here." He tucked a lock of black hair behind his ear.

Mentioning his parents reminded me again of our age difference. I ran a hand down my face, debating if I should send him back to the club since the issue seemed to bother me. I should consider myself lucky he was interested at all. Most guys would kill for the opportunity to be with a younger man, and I was having a moral dilemma. "Old enough to not go to jail" made it seem like he was barely eighteen. Too young. Exactly how he was acting. This was a onetime thing, not a lifelong commitment, I chastised myself and pushed it down. Sin was old enough to know what he was doing.

Minutes later, we pulled up to the hotel and the valet opened the door, letting Sin out first. He stumbled and laughed, a short staccato sound, as he grabbed the valet's jacket, trying to steady himself. I quickly hooked an arm around Sin's waist, stopping him from tumbling just as he'd done for me earlier, and waited until he regained his balance before continuing on.

"I've never stayed at the Roosevelt before," Sin said as we entered the lobby, every step dubious. We moved deeper into the hotel, past the front desk and toward the elevator. "One summer, my family did the whole Universal Studios, Disneyland vacation, and we'd stayed at the Beverly Hills Hotel. But my dad, he's got a condo here for work, somewhere in Century City, I think." He licked his lips and ran his eyes over my body, sending little bits of electricity with his nervous gaze.

I pushed the button to the elevator, and the doors opened immediately. "Your father's business must be quite successful to have a condo here and a home in Nevada."

"Yeah. He's, like, number one at what he does. Keeps him pretty busy." Rolling on his heels and looking up at the elevator's ascending numbers, he clasped his elbows, taking a protective stance. Unsure if his nervousness was from talking about his family or going to a stranger's hotel room, I reminded him he could say no.

"You're so sweet." He seemed to relax for a heartbeat when his eyes met mine. "It's just, last time I did this—go to a stranger's hotel room— it didn't go very well. He wasn't interested once we got to messing around, and I left all hot and bothered."

That assuaged my apprehension; I wasn't the first.

"I promise you," I said, caging him against the wall and brushing my lips against his. "You're going to beg me to let you come." I wedged my thigh between his legs and felt his shaft thicken. "And when I finally give you permission, you're going to scream my name so loudly, the people in the lobby three floors below us will hear you."

"Oh dear lord," Sin whined, the pupils of his eyes growing larger.

The elevator dinged. The smell of new carpet and air freshener failed to hide the lingering funk of sweat and stale air as we walked down the hallway to my corner room. I slid the keycard into the lock and motioned for him to enter first, and flicked on the lights.

Without hesitating, he sat on the bed and removed his high-heeled boots. "I hope you don't mind. These things kill." He flexed his stocking-covered feet a few times.

"Are they new?"

"The whole outfit is, actually. I'm not used to wearing this high of a heel, which you could probably tell since I nearly knocked you over at the club." He examined his surroundings. "These are nice rooms. Small, but nice. And you got a good view of the city." The view was the best thing about the room, which barely fit the queen size bed occupying one side. Opposite the bed was a television mounted on the wall, a writing desk underneath it, and a small coffee table with a high back leather chair facing it. The décor blended together in solid tones of blue-gray, black, and vanilla.

"The doubles are much nicer. This was the only one available tonight under the firm's account." I tossed the keycard onto the desk. "Drink?"

"No, thanks." He hopped off the bed and approached me. "You said the firm paid for the room. Are you an attorney?"

"Yes, is that a problem?"

"Not really." The way he shifted from foot to foot said otherwise.

I curved a finger under his jaw and traced the edge of it with my thumb. He closed his eyes and took a long, slow breath as he leaned into my touch. It reminded me of a cat. "And what is it you do that's left you disgruntled with attorneys?"

"Fuck up." He swallowed hard and looked up at me. A nervous laugh escaped him. "God, that was so extra. I'm sorry. Forget I said it." Sin put his hands on my waist and brought his lips to mine. "It doesn't matter." Obviously it did.

I returned his kisses, though my mind remained anywhere but in the moment.

His comment weighed on me. "Fuck up" was a dramatic answer to tell a complete stranger. But I should be enjoying myself, not diving into pop psychology. Sin was here to fuck, not kick back on the sofa and reveal why he believed he was a fuckup, or why he had a thing against attorneys.

He ran his warm hands under my shirt and lifted it over my head. His hands felt so good. His lips even better. Alternating between soft kisses and licks, he mapped my exposed chest. His touch brought me back to the moment and how much I'd missed this feeling, this closeness with another being. I'd become rock hard with so little effort, and it hadn't gone unnoticed.

"That's impressive." He palmed me, rubbing a few times before unclasping the button on my pants and releasing my cock. "Commando? You are an eager one."

His brown eyes grew wide and he dropped to his knees. Without hesitation, he circled the mushroom tip with his tongue, nudging it into the slit until my cock throbbed with need.

"Fuck, yes," I groaned as he swallowed me until I was deep in his throat. He pushed my pants farther down and dug his nails into my ass as he hollowed his cheeks and bobbed like his life depended on sucking the orgasm from me. The addition of the metal bar rubbing against my sensitive flesh had me on the precipice of coming entirely too soon.

The fucking best head I'd had in ages.

Gently, I pulled him off my cock. Confused and wild-eyed, he looked up at me. His lips were swollen and red, his lipstick smeared along my shaft and his mouth. The sight was sexier than I'd anticipated, a picture I'd keep with me for future lonely nights. Of all the scenes Nic and I had played out, he'd never been into guyliner or dressing in lingerie, something I was grateful for as I indulged myself with Sin.

"Remove your dress."

"Aren't you a bossy one?"

His reply, most likely meant to be flirtatious, came out slightly shaky. Sin showed no apprehension about giving me a blow job, but conversation brought out his nervousness. An interesting twist.

He stood, tugged the stretchy fabric over his head, and discarded it onto a chair. A satin corset thing pushed his flesh together, giving him the illusion of breasts, and a tiny triangle of underwear failed to cover his erect, pierced cock. A Prince Albert.

*Oh, fuck me, that's hot.*

I continued studying his body, taking in the ink on his fair skin. Most prominent were the tattoos on his forearm of a purple and blue lotus combined with waves and words written in cursive— The Wounds are Where the Light Gets In. There appeared to be more tattoos on his left thigh, hidden under his stockings.

Holding his elbows, he quietly stated, "If you want the basque off, I'll need your help."

The lingerie was the hottest thing I'd seen, and it was staying on.

"Not yet." I toed out of my shoes and finished removing my pants. Taking his head in my hands, I placed a soft kiss on his lips. "You're a masterpiece—a remarkable work of art."

I unclasped the stockings from the basque, as he called it, and hooked my fingers around the spaghetti straps of the thong, taking my time as I tugged the scanty fabric down his unshaved legs. His pubic hair, however, was well trimmed.

"Beautiful," I whispered and trailed kisses along the slit of exposed abdomen, feeling his stomach tremble with every placement of my lips. Taking the base of his cock in my hand and pulling back the foreskin, I teased his shaft with my tongue, warming him up for what was to come. Reaching between his legs, I found another surprise—a guiche piercing. Sin was my Paradise, all piercings and tattoos. I fondled the metal, tugging and turning it, as I sucked on his balls.

"Oh, fuck," he said with a throaty moan. His body went taut, his scent grew stronger, hinting that my briefest of ministrations had him close to peaking entirely too soon.

"What do you want, baby?" I clasped his cock, stroking it in a long, lazy rhythm.

"I wanna come in your mouth."

"Maybe later." I gave one final tug and released him.

"Fuck. That's just mean," he groused, his eyes narrowing.

"It'll be worth it. I promise. Get on the bed."

# Chapter Four

Oisin

Trent captivated me with his ocean-blue eyes, brown hair, and designer ginger beard—all physical traits I loved. Especially the ginger beard.

When the Neanderthal had approached us at the bar, I could tell Trent was close to losing it. I knew that man had done him damage. My reaction had been similar when my ex introduced me to her new boyfriend, Karl, or Kody, or some other *K* name. What I hadn't anticipated in my split-second revenge kiss was the magnetic pull of this attractive man. The playful seduction I'd started escalated, like we'd both been set on fire and had to suck face to put it out.

One kiss, and I'd lost my mind. And I was about to lose all my clothes.

I lay facedown on the bed, my breath coming in quick spurts. A sweat broke out across my body as Trent straddled my thighs. I had no idea what I was doing, and in less than a minute, Trent would know, too. I resisted the urge to bolt out the door and embarrass myself. When I shifted, I felt his heavy cock resting at the cleft of my ass, and clenched around it; it seemed huge. Wasn't he supposed to prep me? Lube? Spit?

"Easy, baby. Just relax," he said, massaging my back, alternating between hard and light strokes, and turning me into a puddle of mush.

"Oh God." I moaned as he pressed into a muscle by my shoulder blade. If Trent's kink was to massage his lover, I wanted in.

"Feels good?"

"Amazing," I said as I drooled a little onto the bedcover. Not sexy. He rubbed my thighs, pressing deep into the tight hamstrings. "Oh fuck. Right there." I released a pornworthy groan of approval and chuckled at how ridiculous I sounded over a thigh rub.

"Your ink is fucking sexy." So were those hands tracing my tattoos. "What made you choose this?" He grazed his fingertips along my arm, over a slight alteration of a Rumi quote.

"I got it to help me remember to stay positive, even if everything seems like it's falling apart." Unlike Rumi's intention of being closer to a higher power during dark times, it reminded me that I wasn't alone; there were people who loved me. Especially Devon. Without his love those months after Carrie and I broke up, I might not have made it through.

"Did you design the rest of them?" He stroked my arm, following the muscles from my bicep to my wrist, leaving goose bumps behind.

"No, I have an artist in Vegas who did." I slurred the words, drunk on his touch.

The large ocean scene on my leg had taken a year to complete. It began on my thigh and cascaded down to my calf, portraying a tall ship sailing the ocean while a blue mermaid and giant squid lurked beneath. On my other calf, three lotuses floated on water. The artist had drawn them like a watercolor painting, the pink petals fading into my flesh. I'd never seen more gorgeous work. The artist was brilliant.

"I used to draw when I was younger, and this guy has talent." Trent moved down my body, rubbing my calves and erasing my mind.

"That feels so...oh, yeah. Does this massage come with a happy ending?"

He slid his hands between my thighs and tugged at the ring in my taint. "Very happy," he replied as he circled my hole with a wet finger and nudged inside. The intrusion caused me to clench again. "Relax." A firm hand rested at the small of my back, comforting me. This guy was entirely too perfect.

"Do you take this much time with all your lovers? No, wait. Don't answer that." Why couldn't I just shut up and enjoy this? I spread my legs farther apart, so he could penetrate me more easily. The *snick* of a bottle opening—I had no idea when he'd gotten that—and cool liquid eliminated the burn as he carefully slid between my cheeks, taunting my hole with each pass.

"No," he answered anyway. "I just want to take my time and enjoy you. Make sure you can take me." He slipped inside, pushing past that tight ring, and worked another finger—fingers—inside me, spreading me farther.

I thanked every deity I could think of for his expertise when he angled his long fingers just right. An odd noise bleated from me, somewhere between a whimper and plea. So embarrassing.

"That's it. Let me hear you. Don't be shy," he coaxed, continuing to rub inside me.

I writhed against the bed, seeking friction. Unsatisfied, I reached for my cock.

"No, I want to feel you pulse around me when I'm buried deep in you." Trent slowly withdrew his fingers. The sound of a condom package being torn caused my heart to race.

This was it. If I didn't stop him now, he was going to fuck me.

I watched as he slid the condom over his anaconda. How the hell was that going to fit inside me?

"Deep breath, baby," he coached as he rubbed that monster between my cheeks. Instinctively, I tensed. "You can take it."

I did as he said. The blunt tip slid in and...no pain and only a modicum of burn. He continued massaging my upper back and arms, not pushing deeper inside me, giving me time to adjust. Trent was a considerate lover, and I doubted I could've found a better man than him for my first time bottoming.

"Are you ready?" Desire drenched his voice.

"Yes." I clenched around him as I anticipated a thrust.

"Tell me you want me to fuck you."

Interesting kink. "I want you to fuck me." Saying it out loud unexpectedly set my body on fire.

"Good boy," he praised, and I imagined him smiling, pleased that I'd obeyed him. He could command me to do anything at this point, and I'd be all for it as long as it meant he'd fuck me. "Get on all fours." He was breathless, as if he was finally losing some of his calm control. He pulled me up by the hips, staying lodged within me.

"Yes, Sir," I replied jokingly.

Sweat trickled down my back as Trent worked every inch into my tightness. I'd never been happier for lube in my life. He was thick...like two-dicks thick, or at least it felt that way. I was, as Devon put it, an ass virgin. What did I know? Maybe this was normal. It hurt. It felt amazing. And I couldn't wait to feel him fucking me. His balls finally rested against me, and that was when he lightly pushed me down, pressing my chest flat on the mattress and angling my ass high in the air.

"So fucking tight," he crooned, rubbing his hands down my waist. The darn basque acted as a barrier between the flesh of his hands and my body.

"Please. Please fuck me." I rocked my hips back slowly moving along his shaft, urging him to take over. And boy did he...

He fucked me, hard. Fingers dug into my hips, guaranteeing bruises to be savored later. All my focus was on the dick impaling me, the primal way he maneuvered me on his cock. I decided I loved bottoming—letting someone take care of me. I'd always been good to my lovers, which I didn't mind at all, but this? Having Trent work me over, relax me, and then fuck me? Absolute nirvana, and exactly what I needed. Moaning, panting, and a litany of unintelligible pleas and yeses spilled uncontrollably from me. My brain melted into a pool on the mattress.

Trent placed his arm across my chest and pulled me onto his lap, torso to back, while I remained on his cock. "Lean back." I did, resting my head on his shoulder, and watched as he poured lube along my shaft. The firm grip gliding up and down my length, combined with being stuffed with cock, had me feeling pretty slutty in the best of ways. "I'm deep inside you, so fucking deep. You're so sexy like this, here in my arms, letting me fuck you." He kissed my neck, nipping the skin. "Tell me when you're close."

"I'm close!" Barely three strokes in, and I clenched around his dick, staving off the tingling pressure as my balls drew higher.

"Ask permission." The low, commanding tone caused me to shudder. I was at his mercy and having to ask if I could come? Yeah, I totally got into that.

"Can...I...please...come?" I asked between each powerful stroke of his hand. It took everything I had not to erupt. This need to please him, to get him to praise me again, forced me to resort to images of lima beans and granny pants so I didn't shoot my load.

"Say, 'Can I please come, Sir.'"

*Seriously?* I didn't know what kind of game he was playing and didn't fucking care. I was so turned on I'd do just about anything to get off. "Can...I...please...come, Sir?"

"Yeah. I want you to fucking come so hard. Give me everything."

Lightning struck my spine, my stomach launched skyrockets, and I floated in space. I barely noticed Trent spanking the side of my ass as I shot my load. If anything, the pain intensified my orgasm.

"Such a good boy." His praise electrified me, causing my dick to pulse again. The world shifted as he pushed me down on my stomach again and pounded into me. He thrust a final time and froze, releasing what was possibly the hottest sound I'd heard someone make when they came. *Dang.* He rested briefly on my back, catching his breath before pulling out.

My body was a useless pile of jelly. I'd never come so freaking hard in my life and the power of it had me drifting into sleep. While I lay half-awake, Trent removed my basque—finally—and cleaned me up. He pulled the covers down and motioned for me to get under. I hadn't planned on staying the night, but there was no way I could move. Or function. Or think. Moments later, I felt his arms wrap around me, holding me so I was against his chest facing him, intimate like lovers. I let myself imagine we were, as I drifted off to sleep.

I WOKE UP in bed alone, feeling completely used and sore in the best of ways. The sheets were warm. He hadn't been gone long. The shower kicked on and a sprig of happiness grew inside me. He'd stayed. I'd get a chance to say goodbye, maybe exchange numbers. Maybe we'd have a chance at something more than a one-night stand.

*Next thing you know, you'll be picking out china patterns. Stop it.*

What that man did to me the previous night could definitely be defined as the best lay I'd ever gotten. He'd held me all night, too. I'd nuzzled in his arms, a little spoon to his big spoon. The ache for something more had dissipated while I drifted in and out of sleep with him beside me.

I threaded my fingers through my hair, dislodging a few stray bobby pins. The hair net and wig lay on the floor, sprawled out like a black octopus. Next them rested the basque, thong, and stockings. The mess reminded me of the ton of makeup I'd worn and how, after all the sweating and fucking, I might now look like Pennywise the hooker.

Tossing the covers aside, I wondered if I should join Trent in the shower. Before I could move, though, he entered the bedroom wearing a towel around his waist and a small grin. Compact and muscular, more athletic than bulky, Trent was hellasexy standing there with his wet brown hair and damp skin. There should be a law against being that hot, really.

"Good morning, sleepy."

I buried my face in my hands and mumbled, "I must look hideous."

"That's a strange greeting." He chuckled. The bed dipped as he sat beside me, smelling deliciously of citrus soap, and pulled my hands away. "You look sated." He rubbed his thumb along my jaw and pressed his lips to mine. I opened for him, tasting toothpaste and him. A whimper escaped me. Fuck. His kiss went right to my toes, my groin, and set me on fire. I started to shift, to straddle him. My ass was so sore and I didn't care. I wanted him inside me again. Before I could move, he pulled away from me wearing an expression mixed with desire and resistance.

"I have to work, otherwise I'd be all for more playtime with you. Stay as long as you want. Breakfast is on the table. I didn't know what you liked, so I ordered pancakes, fruit, eggs, toast, and coffee." He stood and picked up articles of clothing off the floor, dressing as he went along.

"You're so nice," I said, barely audible. I hadn't had many overnight hookups—both of them were before I'd met my ex—and they were of the wham, bam, fuck you and be gone variety. There was no cuddling afterward, no breakfast waiting when I woke up, no kisses or gentle caresses. They were a means to a climax. Trent's generosity and gentleness was foreign and had my stupid heart diving back into that fantasy of picking out china patterns. Cuddling all night added to that fairy tale.

Now completely dressed, Trent returned and sat beside me with something akin to sadness and longing in his eyes. Maybe I just saw what I wanted. "I have to go." He kissed me. Sweet, tender, lips on lips, nothing dirty, just genuine affection that split my heart in half. *Can I keep you?* I stopped myself from pulling him back into bed and begging him to screw me into the mattress. He obviously had things to do, and I didn't want to make him late. Or be rejected.

With a heavy sigh, he got up. "I've left the number of the limo service on the table. Call them when you want to go home." He leaned in and kissed me, cupping my face as he did and turning my insides all fluttery. "I really don't want to go," he added with another kiss. This one felt desperate, like he needed this connection, this intimacy between us as much as I did. "I could stay here and fuck you all day, and it still wouldn't enough."

"Then do it." I hated the neediness in my voice, that I sounded so pathetic. Everything about him leaving was wrong.

"Goodbye, Sin." Watching him head toward the door caused me irrational pain. I ached. My heart, my body.

"Trent, wait." I got up, forgetting I was completely naked, and went to him.

"Damn, you are just so fucking gorgeous." He swiped the corner of his mouth as his eyes raked my body.

"Um, could we do this again? I mean, it doesn't have to be serious or anything. I'm in town for the weekend. I had a really good time, and I think you did too and..."

He palmed my chin and I nestled into the smoothness, closing my eyes. I felt his breath on my face before his lips met mine. He made me feel delicate. Worthy. Precious. Every delicious flick of his tongue, every lusty nip of his teeth, and every tender press of his lips led me to think he'd felt the same soul connection. There was one thing I was certain about: Trent had ruined me for anyone else.

"Give me your phone."

I scrambled, looking for the small purse I'd carried and found it hooked over the back of the leather chair. I retrieved my phone and handed it to him.

"Text me tonight." He entered his digits.

A man that gorgeous, attentive, and that stellar a kisser was like a unicorn. A unicorn that wanted me.

"I will," I promised, my heart perched somewhere between disbelief and hope.

"I look forward to it." He gave me another kiss. This time it was deep, dirty, and absolutely greedy. "I really do have to leave now. I wish I could stay here and fuck you all over again." With another sigh and a goodbye, Trent left the room.

"Holy shit," I said to no one.

The only person I had to share my good fortune with was Devon, and I immediately texted my BFF. He'd already sent five texts asking how the night had gone, so I wasn't surprised when the phone rang instantly.

"How was he?" Devon cut right to the point. That was typical Devon, though.

"Fucking amazing. Oh my God. Just...wow."

"It's about time, Os. I'm happy for you. You still at the Roosevelt?"

"Yeah." I went into the bathroom to see the damage. I looked well used. My eye makeup was smudged, lipstick worn off, and my brown hair stuck out in all directions. I was also covered in lube and sperm despite the cleaning up Trent did. "I look rode hard and put away wet. I need a shower." I laughed, not sure if I should be mortified Trent had seen me like this or elated that he had and still wanted to hook up. One thing I knew, getting back into the previous night's outfit was not going to happen. "Could you come get me and bring a change of clothes?"

"Stone and I will be by in about twenty minutes."

After ending the call, I checked the remainder of my messages and saw one from Paws for Love. *Maggie.* A jolt of anxiety ticked my pulse up a few notches as I listened to the voicemail from Dr. Parker.

"I got the results back early from the biopsy, and Maggie is fine. The tumor was benign. I'm keeping her at the hospital this weekend to let her rest, and then I'll bring her home on Monday. If you're around, come by and visit. Have a good weekend."

"Yes!" I fist pumped the air. The fleabag was gonna be okay. I couldn't believe my fortune. Maggie was healthy. I had another night with Trent lined up, and Dev and I were going to Universal Studios later. What a fantastic weekend!

I jumped in the shower, singing and scrubbing, learning just how much false eyelashes hurt when peeled off. I took care of my morning wood, imagining Trent fucking me all over. The image had me shooting my load in under a minute—record time. I dried off and secured the towel around my waist, unable to stop smiling as I dove into the pancake breakfast, complete with scrambled eggs and hot coffee. The edge of a business card peaked out from the carafe of orange juice. I recognized the limo company as one my father used.

A pricking sensation trekked down my spine.

I was sure lots of highbrow clientele used them, not just my father's firm. This was Hollywood, after all. It had to be a coincidence.

Using my phone, I went to the website and searched the company directory of Harrison, Preston, and Bryant, Inc., Los Angeles. My stomach wound tighter than a cobra about to strike and threatened to purge my breakfast as I stared at a younger clean-shaven version of Trent with preppy-short brown hair. His name and specialties were listed beside the photo.

Trenton Fisher IP, Talent and Professional Sports Contracts.

Fuck.

I had the worst luck.

# Chapter Five

TRENTON

The empty garage at my new place of employment provided evidence that this was indeed Saturday, and I should have a life outside of work. A silver Lexus LS was parked in one of the company's executive spots by the elevator, an odd comfort that I wasn't the only one lacking a social life. I pulled into a spot next to it, feeling unfulfilled by the conquest. Parking in Century City, I'd have had to prowl like a big cat to find a spot and be equally as stealthy to cut other drivers off to get it. Not in Vegas, not even during the week that I'd been here.

I trudged into the elevator, latte in hand, and rode it to the seventh floor, ready to slog through my predecessor's caseload.

Overall, the move had been swift, which had been mandatory since I'd only had two weeks to do so after the record release party. I'd left most of my personal effects in my West Hollywood condo, knowing I'd be shuttling back and forth for at least the next three months, and shipped the essentials to the fully furnished three-bedroom home the company had leased for me. Lots of space. Lizards. Sand. Moving did nothing but remind me how lonely my life had become, how work ate up every free minute. But that wouldn't happen here. I had family to visit, and they'd make damn sure I did. Initially, I dreaded the distraction. Now, I viewed them as the kick in the pants I needed to get out of a vicious cycle of all work and no play.

When the elevator doors opened, the deserted sea of cubicles greeted me and the motion sensor lights flickered on, casting the whole place with an eerie vibe. Seldom had I been alone like this in the California branch, and I missed the commotion. This environment felt as soulless as my rented house in the desert. Barren. Much like my love life. The last person I'd been with was Sin, and despite the amazing sex we had, he never contacted me.

If he texted me right now and asked to meet, I'd jump at the chance. I'd grown intrigued by him. I couldn't forget his coy smile, the way he tasted or felt, the lyrical moans that poured out of his mouth while I fucked him. And I loved waking up next to him nestled in my arms, his warm body pressed against mine. We'd fit perfectly together. I tried not to pine away for him like some lovesick teenager, but he'd gotten under my skin.

Harrison's office door was open a crack, and I could hear his muffled voice seething with anger. He kept his head most of the time. Whoever had angered him to this level was worthy of such hostility. I'd always thought he flew to Vegas on the weekends to spend time with his family, not deal with work at this branch. I quickly passed his office and slipped into mine, not wanting to disturb him or be a part of whatever hostility was taking place.

The midsize office I'd inherited had a full wall of floor-to-ceiling windows and was decorated in a style more befitting a grandfather than a young attorney. An oppressive cherrywood desk occupied nearly the entire length of a common wall, and opposite it was a dark leather sofa that showed little wear and a coffee table with matching end table.

I missed the contemporary flair of my office in California.

"It's temporary," I reminded myself.

I'd barely touched the power button on my computer when my desk phone buzzed.

"Fisher," Harrison's deep timbre vibrated through the speaker. "I'd like you to come to my office." He hung up without waiting for a reply. That conversation must have hitched his blood pressure to astronomic heights.

I stood outside Harrison's office listening to him continue to reprimand the poor sod in there.

"I can't believe you had the nerve to come into this firm with a hangover and looking like you just rolled out of bed. You think you can party it up and still pass law school? Your performance is disastrous, Oisin, and if you think I'll stand for this, you are mistaken. Being my son doesn't grant you privilege or immunity. You have to earn your place just like everyone else."

"Yes, Dad," a weary voice answered.

"You'll assist Mr. Fisher today, and I expect you to give him a hundred and ten percent. Understood?"

"Yes."

I'd never met Harrison's sons, only his wife. He kept a few family portraits in his office, and I knew his eldest had gotten a degree in the arts, while his youngest son was pursuing a Juris Doctor. Judging by his father's hostile tone, he wasn't doing well.

I waited for a lull in conversation to knock. Footsteps approached, and the door opened.

"Come in, Fisher," Harrison said and motioned to the other figure in the room. "This is my son, Oisin." He pronounced his name "ocean," and my unbridled, cheesy first thought was how much I'd like to dive into the young man. Despite his sleep-deprived and completely disheveled appearance, Oisin Harrison was gorgeous. He wore black-rimmed glasses that complimented his square-shaped face, giving him a hipster flair. The bangs of his dark brown hair swept to one side in emo fashion while the rest of his hair was a disaster, as if he'd run his hands through it a million times. He was dressed in crumpled layers of black and white. The chaotic mess only made him more attractive.

"Nice to meet you," I said, extending my hand.

He rose from his seat and inhaled sharply when he looked at me—a curious response—and paused, seemingly stunned, before accepting my hand. "Likewise," he rasped. This kid looked nothing like the smiling, conventionally dressed teen in the photos Harrison had in his office. He sat back down gingerly, holding on to his side. Harrison failed to comment on it, making me wonder if they'd already addressed that issue before my arrival.

"Have a seat." Harrison leaned against his desk and motioned for me to take the plush chair next to his son. "Fisher was top of his class and his study teams at Harvard. He passed both the California bar and Nevada bar the first time around."

I admit I was proud of those accomplishments. Most people had to take the California bar exam several times before passing. It was a bitch. I wasn't sure where the review of my qualifications was heading, though, and it had me concerned. If Oisin was failing law school, there was no need to rub my success in his face.

"Dad, you don't have to do this." Oisin took off his glasses and rubbed his eyes. "I'll get help at the university."

"That's right you will," Harrison snapped. Crossing his arms he addressed me. "Fisher, I have an unusual request. Oisin has been slacking off his first year of law school, and he needs someone to bring him up to speed. I believe he could benefit from your expertise and real-world experience, not to mention your excellent people skills—something my son lacks. I know this deviates from your job description, but I was hoping you'd consider."

*How the fuck do I get out of this?*

"Sir, not to be disrespectful, but the tutors at the university would be better equipped."

"I'll be arranging that for him as well. I'm certain if he sees how you put into practice what he's supposed to be learning, you'll inspire him to do better."

"And he wants someone to keep an eye on me," Oisin muttered, slowly shifting in his seat as he put his glasses back on.

"I wouldn't have to keep an eye on you if you were mature and responsible enough to know better than to piss your life away," Harrison countered and turned his attention back to me. "He'd meet with you in the office once a week for a few hours to go over his assignments. I won't hold you accountable if Oisin continues to fail. All I'm asking is for you to act as a mentor. He needs guidance. And Fisher, I've never had a more dedicated, passionate employee than you."

Harrison seldom doled out such praise. He was trusting me to help his son, a testament to his faith in my abilities. Still, I couldn't help but feel curious as to why I'd been chosen as babysitter. Yes, I'd been a TA in college and had excelled in law school. But with the kind of money Harrison had, he could've gotten Oisin a full-time tutor at the university. Something didn't add up.

If this was another hoop I had to jump through to make partner, I had to say yes.

"I'll do what I can to help you," I said to Oisin, who sucked on his bottom lip as a response. *Fuck, that's sexy.*

"Thank you, Fisher. I'm sure the two of you will manage without me. I promised Angel brunch." Harrison buttoned his suit jacket and stepped toward his son to place a hand on his shoulder. "You can reach me on my cell," he added before leaving Oisin and me alone.

Oisin slumped, tension releasing in his shoulders and his face. "What do you need me to do?" he asked, running a hand through his unkempt hair. The despondent look in those hazel eyes said he'd given up. Burned out at what—twenty-two, twenty-three years old? I'd seen it happen to a few of my classmates, the ones who quit law school within the first year. Did Oisin Harrison's decision to pursue a law career have more to do with his father's wishes than his own?

"There are several files on my desk. Make sure the most current information is in the computer system and then file them. If there are any pressing dates, please make note of them and mark them in the calendar." It was bullshit work I hated to do and nothing that my paralegal couldn't finish on Monday.

"Yes, sir."

I bristled at those two familiar words, hoping like hell that tenor voice was not the same tenor voice I'd had moaning my name in a Los Angeles hotel a couple weeks ago. It couldn't be. *Yeah, it could.* The dots lined up, but made no sense. As Oisin slowly shuffled past me, holding his side and obviously in pain, I filed the thought away. Going there would have implications I wasn't ready to acknowledge.

How had Harrison not seen that he was hurting? If Nic had displayed that type of discomfort, I'd have ordered him to see a doctor and then to bed. The thought of Nic gripped my stomach. I'd let work take precedence over our relationship, never seeing the end coming until it was too late. The comparison between Harrison's neglect for his son and my neglect for my former lover glared at me.

I returned to my office and found Oisin gathering the bulky legal files. I took them from him and placed them back on my desk. "I've changed my mind. I've got something else for you to do."

"Sir?"

"Do you see that couch over there?"

"Yes."

"Get some sleep."

"Why?"

"I don't know what the heck is going on between you and your father, and I certainly don't want to be in the middle of it. But here I am—your mentor." I added finger quotes around mentor. "You won't gain anything from mundane data entry, and in your present state, you'll be lucky if you can enter it correctly. You look exhausted, and I can't believe your father didn't send you home." I'd let my frustration show. I shouldn't have. I had more respect for Harrison than to think he'd intentionally dismissed his son's condition, and my comment made it sound like I'd taken sides. I guess I had.

"You don't know anything about me. Don't assume I'd screw up just because I'm tired." His voice wavered as he spoke, as if it took considerable strength to confront me. "And as for my dad, he's preoccupied. My parents..." He rubbed the back of his neck, looking down at his feet. "Never mind."

I sat on the corner of my desk. Softening my tone, I said, "I didn't mean to offend you. Forgive me."

"Thanks." Oisin remained fixated on his boots, lost in thought. "I wish you didn't work for him," he mumbled.

"Excuse me?"

"Nothing, sorry. I, uh..." He bit his bottom lip, sucking on it for a second before releasing it. I flashed back to Sin—the way he raked his teeth across his lip piercing.

"Jana can handle all of this on Monday. Why don't you go home and rest? Or if you're worried about going home because of your dad, my offer stands. You can sleep on the couch until I leave for lunch."

He glanced over at the leather sofa. "Are you sure? I-I don't really want to go back to my apartment."

"Absolutely." I'd have felt better taking him to a doctor to check that side he kept favoring, but Harrison asked me to be a mentor, not a mother hen.

He eased himself down on the couch. "Are you the only one coming in today?"

"As far as I know, yes. I don't keep tabs on the others, though." I sat behind my desk and powered up my laptop. "Why?"

He fidgeted with his hands. "I don't want to get you into trouble."

Him worrying about me was adorable. "I appreciate the concern. If anyone bothers me about you being in my office, I'll handle it."

A small smile. "Thank you." He removed his glasses, set them on the coffee table, and lay down on his left side, expelling an audible breath.

"Need some painkillers or something?"

"No, the doctor gave me some superstrength ibuprofen."

So he had gone to the doctor. That alleviated some of my concern. I wanted to ask what his diagnosis was, but he'd already closed his eyes.

I went through my emails. Soon, I was immersed in answering questions and reading proposed contracts, making sure all negotiated points had been addressed and fine-tuning the rest. Three hours later, the rumbling in my stomach alerted me it was time for lunch.

I glanced over to Oisin—still sleeping, mouth parted. His head rested on his arm, and his messy brown hair splayed every which way. The lack of tension on his face enhanced his boyish appearance, reminding me of our age difference, yet I couldn't stop staring. An exposed area of skin just below his belly button from where his long-sleeve shirt had ridden up caught my attention. My dick twitched as I thought about touching him there, unbuttoning his pants, and freeing that bulge. He was well endowed, and those tight pants were excellent advertisement.

"Do you like what you see?" Oisin asked.

Damn. I'd been caught.

"You looked peaceful and I didn't want to wake you, but I'm leaving for the day." I turned away to straighten out some already meticulous files on my desk, scolding myself for checking out my boss's son. After finishing with the files, I closed my laptop.

Oisin stood with his arms wrapped around his sides, seeming not so much in pain as perhaps insecurity. "Do you think you could give me a ride to my apartment? It's not that far from here. I took a taxi earlier." He had striking eyes. Light brown surrounded his pupils while pale blue filled his irises, swirling like mini spiral galaxies. Looking away, he picked up his glasses from the table and effectively snapped me out of his orbit.

"No problem." I packed up my laptop and stared at the files I should take home, thinking they could wait until Monday. My hesitation to work was new and should've set off warning bells. With the promise of partnership so close, I shouldn't give up or slack off. Reluctantly, I stuffed the paperwork in the pouch of my bag. I'd review it later after dinner with my family. "Ready?"

Oisin nodded and walked ahead of me, giving me a nice view of his pert ass. I groaned internally. This boy had me all worked up, underscoring my need to get laid. Or jack off. Regardless, fucking my boss's son would be a horrible career move.

"You coming?" He turned around, catching me staring again.

I was a terrible person.

"I'll meet you at the elevator." I had to get my head together. Harrison wanted me to mentor his son, not eye-fuck him. I waited a few seconds, collecting myself before shutting the lights off in my office, and followed Oisin into the elevator. Determined not to stare inappropriately at him, I fixated on the descending numbers, trying to ignore the heat radiating off his body as he stood ridiculously close to me. The faint scent of his cologne and sweat made me want to lick his flesh.

"Are you okay?"

"Fine." I clutched the strap of my bag tighter. "Low blood sugar, that's all. I'll be better after I eat lunch."

I swear he smirked.

# Chapter Six

OISIN

Fate was messing with me. I'd expected the verbal lashing of my father. I hadn't expected to listen to it with sore ribs after a night out that had gone terribly wrong, and I certainly didn't expect Trenton Fisher, the man I'd tried to forget, to be assigned to babysitting duties. Dad must have been completely desperate to sic Trent, one of his star attorneys, on me. I may have deleted Trent's number, but I couldn't stop myself from searching his name online. He had no social media to creep. Everything available was career related. I found articles that mentioned him with a well-known basketball player and others that showed his affiliation with Mutant Militia. I also may have accidentlly on purpose bumped into Thomas Bryant's paralegal and inquired about Trent for a friend of mine who was looking for a good attorney.

When Trent shook my hand in the office, he gave no indication he recognized me from the club. Then again, I had barely recognized me with all that makeup—especially with it smeared across my face. And that day at the office, I'd had my glasses on and no brown contacts and looked like the emo kid who'd partied too hard, a far cry from the Goth chick that Trent met weeks ago.

And now, here I was in an elevator with him. I should've called Devon for a ride and not jumped at the chance to spend more time with Trent, who'd been checking me out all day. He'd arched an eyebrow while looking at my ass. He'd stared at my groin. I'd caught him both times and resisted the urge to tell him who I was, that he'd already had me on all fours, that he'd already made me come so many times I couldn't function for days afterward. My dad, when boasting about how I needed some guidance, had said Mr. Fisher was an exemplary lawyer and was in line for a junior partnership position. Mr. Trenton Fisher could probably kiss that goodbye if he boned his boss's son.

I fidgeted with my hands the entire elevator ride. Lack of sleep and a touch of a hangover couldn't stop my mind from racing, and Trent standing so close had me fighting the urge to snuggle into him—among other less G-rated things—and forget about this bad day.

Dad made it clear all of his employees were hands off after Carrie and I broke up. She'd been a paralegal at the firm when we'd met and quit after we called off the engagement. Dad had scolded me, saying I shouldn't date anyone from his firm because it effected his business and reputation, that people would see me as a shortcut to a promotion or assume they'd receive favor because they were with his son—things he never mentioned when Carrie and I first began to date, or later when we got engaged.

No matter what reason he gave, I suspected he had a hard time accepting both his sons liked men. Much like Carrie, my father failed to understand the concept of bisexuality, and after seeing Devon and me together during our dating phase, I think when I proposed to Carrie, my dad believed he'd hit the straight-son jackpot. His letdown had been monumental.

We exited the elevator, and the chirp of the key fob revealed Trent's car was a black Audi A7, probably worth about eighty grand.

"Nice ride," I said, slipping onto the tan leather seat and admiring all the fancy gadgets on the console. The smell of leather and new car lingered, and the seats hugged my butt. Cars weren't my thing. I had a beat up Bimmer that spent more time in the shop than on the road lately. Thankfully, my BFF was a killer mechanic and the reason why I knew anything at all about this Audi.

"Thanks. I got it last year as a sort of pick-me-up."

"Most people buy ice cream or chocolate when they're down. You must have needed some serious picking up."

"I did." He started the car and backed out without elaborating.

The drive to my apartment was quiet—a break from the noise of life and the pressure of everything external. I studied Trent's handsome profile as he navigated through the streets leading away from the office and toward the edge of suburbia. Strong nose, thin lips, ginger beard. He wasn't one of those guys you'd look at and say, damn he's fashion model worthy. But he was intense. He was nerdy hot. And when not in lawyer mode, he was flammable sex. Trenton Fisher was the kind of man that hit all my buttons and exactly the reason why I risked going to the hotel with him in the first place.

His jaw tightened, eyes fixed on the road but not wholly focused on driving. No one drove with that much intensity unless they were in the Indy 500 or something.

"Everything okay?"

"I was just thinking about you, honestly." He sent me an apologetic glance.

"Really?" I tried to quiet the pounding of my heart. *Wild monkey sex would be good.*

"You've been favoring your side all day."

Oh, that. "Not much to tell. I went out last night and got too wasted. Next thing I knew, these guys were kicking the shit out of me and then took off." I left out the fact I knew one of the guys personally, that he'd recently graduated from UNLV's law school. He hadn't appreciated my blow job skills the way Trent had.

"Are you going to report it?"

"It's this left up here," I directed him. "Um, no."

I had no intention of reporting it. Kyle Hernandez, the kid I'd sucked off in the bathroom—a first and last time for me—was well connected in the Nevada justice system. His parents were both district attorneys. Between them and my father, I imagined the case would turn into a three-ring circus, rendering me the poster boy for LGBT crimes and highlighting the unwillingness of victims of said hate crimes to come forward. The shoe fit, but I didn't want to wear it. Besides, my classmates hated me already, and going public about what I did behind closed bathroom stall doors was nobody's business. Being the son of a legendary lawyer made law school and my personal life a special kind of hell.

Trent grunted, leaving me to guess if he approved or not. "If you want to talk about it, or change your mind, let me know."

"Thanks, but I'm okay." The only person I'd told was Devon. He'd been the one to take me to the twenty-four hour urgent care and drive me to the firm. He would've stayed with me all day and blown off work if I'd asked. Instead, I agreed to give him a call after I received penance from dear old dad.

We'd reached the cluster of student apartments without saying anything more. The weathered two-storied place attempted to be hip, painted three different shades of brown with steel railings protecting the small porches off of each unit. From the seat in Trent's luxury car, where I lived seemed like a compound. "This is the place. You can just pull over here, and I'll jump out. Parking is a pain."

I went to open the door, and Trent lightly grabbed my wrist. Those hands. There was a sizzle, a burst of heat where our flesh met.

"Oisin, I mean it. If you need anything—someone to talk to, just to hang out, or whatever—I'd like to give you my number. Call me whenever, okay?"

I swallowed hard, caught in those blue orbs. "You don't have to pretend to care, Trent. My dad put you in an unfair position. The good part is he said he wouldn't hold you accountable if I don't improve. So you can just tell him I blew you off, and do your job instead of babysitting me." Maybe if I pushed him away, I could be free of him. Unlikely.

Trent kept his hand on mine. I liked the contact. I craved it, actually. Loneliness wore on me and was one of the reasons I'd gone out the previous night. I'd give anything to be in Trent's arms again and feel those hands on my body, enveloped in the illusion of love and warmth.

"It has nothing to do with your father, I promise you." He released my hand. "Take my number, anyway."

I pulled out my phone and gave it to him. There'd be no deleting his number this time. When he finished, he handed it back, and I got out of the car.

"My office Wednesday at six?" he asked.

An "Okay" spilled from my mouth before my brain could stop it. Having a little bit of Trent's attention, even if we couldn't be together, was better than nothing.

"See you then."

"See you then," I repeated and shut the car door.

I watched like a lovesick idiot as he drove away.

# Chapter Seven

TRENTON

After dropping Oisin off at his apartment, I checked my messages. My sister Melissa, the eldest of the twins, left an annoyed voicemail about my lack of visiting or calling my family. Mom also had called and the "I know you're busy, sweetie, but when you get a chance I'd love to see you" had me feeling like a heel. I'd forgotten to call and confirm Sunday dinner at her house and immediately remedied that.

"Hi sweetie, are you coming on Sunday for dinner?" my mother asked in her strong Bostonian accent. We'd moved to Vegas when I was a kid, after Dad left us. She'd said we were better without him. With the little bits I remembered of my father—bottle in hand, lots of shouting—I agreed.

"I'll be there. Sorry I didn't call sooner, I—"

"I know how busy you are with work and the move." Mom meant it, too. There was no bitterness in her voice, which made me feel like an egocentric asshole. I'd been relying on my sisters to keep her company while I went off to California, not visiting or calling her as often as I should have. She was getting older, not frail, but I should have made a better effort to stay in touch. I vowed to do so, promotion or not.

We chatted about work and the move, and she told me about the latest stock market trends. Following them was a hobby of hers, and it'd earned her a small fortune for retirement.

"It'll be so good to have all my kids here. I can't wait to see you."

"I'll see you at one on Sunday, Mom. Love you."

"Love you, too," she said and hung up.

Since I was on a familial roll and stuck in lunchtime traffic, I decided to call Melissa back.

"Is this really my long-lost brother? The big shot lawyer who never returns phone calls unless he gets to charge by the minute?" Melissa answered with the deeply sarcastic tone I'd come to associate with her.

I laughed. "The very one."

"I thought I'd lost you in the void of legal backlog."

"It was touch and go, but you'll be happy to know I've arranged a lunch date with Queen Mum for Sunday Brunch, and your family's presence is requested," I added with an arrogant flair.

She snorted a laugh. "We'll be there. Mom's done nothing but talk about how excited she is that you're back in town. Well, that and her usual 'I wish he'd settle down' speech."

"I'm not exactly marriage material. I'm too busy," I grumbled.

"It's not for everyone, but I do remember you being pretty happy with a certain someone."

"How's the veterinary clinic doing?" I attempted to dodge the topic of my love life. Melissa always brought it up and a blind date usually followed.

"Subtle, Trent. Subtle," she said with a chuckle. "I'm not dropping the relationship thing just yet. Since your schedule is so busy, I took the liberty of setting you up on a lunch date on Monday."

*Here we go.* "Melissa, I—"

"Much like my three-year-old daughter, I don't understand the word no. You will be going."

"What's his name?" I resigned.

She squealed with excitement. "He's younger. Graduated top of his class with a degree in biology, a little emo, has a pierced lip—you like that, I remember, or at least you did when you were going through your My Chem phase—and he's very smart. He's great with animals, so I think he'll manage you just fine." The suspicious giggle that followed was the telltale sign of a sister up to no good. "You're going to love him."

"Cocky much?"

"Just enough to bust your tiny balls. By the way, you're meeting at Thai Kitchen. I made the reservation under 'gingerbread man.'" She snickered. I used to love the childhood story to the point of embarrassment, something I'd never lived down. Every Christmas, I received gingerbread-men cookies and themed gifts.

"Could you be any more evil? Gingerbread man and Thai Food?" Thai food and I didn't agree. I liked it. It didn't like me. "And you expect me to show up for this blind date?" I loved my sister too much not to follow through on one of her efforts to make me happy. No matter how much I might like this smart, younger man, I had no desire to date. I clenched my jaw as the image of Sin popped into my mind. Being with him had been exhilarating. I had no inclination toward the fairer sex, but the way Sin had looked in that silky thong, with his pierced cock springing up over the edge—delicious. The smeared lipstick and makeup added a whole other level of dirty hot I could get into. Fuck. I wanted that. I wanted him and his tight little ass—needed to feel his lips wrapped around my cock. The mere thought of it had my dick standing at half-mast. This blind date didn't stand a chance.

"I'll be looking forward to your butt-kissing thank you. You're gonna owe me." Melissa's happiness was palpable.

"I'll see you at Mom's tomorrow."

"Can't wait."

Me neither.

I pulled into the garage of my cookie-cutter home. The houses in the neighborhood resembled each other so closely, I had to double-check the number the first few times to figure out where I lived. Similar in size and design, the desert-themed homes were upscale and their xeriscaping well maintained. The whole place was magazine cover perfect and entirely too quiet. I'd grown used to dirty streets and the noise of traffic and the people living below my West Hollywood condo. I had trouble sleeping here, without the buzzing car alarms or drunk people laughing, just coyotes and crickets.

The inside of the house was pristine, most likely built in the '90s or early 2000s. The kitchen and bathrooms had been remodeled with the newest of stainless-steel appliances. The living areas were open with picturesque views of the red mountains to the west. It was a house, not a home.

I trudged into the downstairs office and plopped my satchel on the desk. After microwaving something questionable for lunch, I turned on the television for company and retreated into the office where I worked steadily until nightfall. Defeat came when I'd read the same paragraph fifteen times, my mind fighting the loneliness surrounding me. There were no ghosts of Nic, no memories of us within these walls to keep me company. It might not have been much, but now that those reminders were gone the void consumed me.

I gave up working and poured a shot of whiskey. Drinking alone was pathetic. But drinking and dialing my friend Georgia? Now that was perfect.

"Sugar! Y'all are psychic, I swear. I was about to call you. I just got into Vegas for the sex convention and am in the mood for a little partying. You down?"

I swirled the whiskey in my glass. "Why the heck not?"

"There's my boy!"

"It's been awhile since I've been your boy, Georgia."

"Hmm, don't I know it," she said adding her infectious cackle. "Those were good days." They were. "I'll text you the place. See you there!"

She hung up before I could say goodbye. Didn't matter. Any place was better than hanging around here in all this…emptiness.

# Chapter Eight

OISIN

My one bedroom apartment wasn't much. It had a small living room with a couch, a desk, and TV, and an even tinier kitchen. If it weren't for the breakfast bar, there'd be no place to eat. When I got home, I ignored the massive pile of material on my desk that I needed to catch up on before the next day's study group and went straight to my bedroom. My bed called to me. I stepped out of my shoes and got under the covers, noting the pain in my ribs had gotten better. Nothing was broken. Just sore. I'd be fine in a few days, thanks to the hulk-like man who had stopped Kyle and his friends from inflicting more damage. I didn't want to wake up for the rest of the weekend, possibly the entire week.

Too bad I forgot to turn my phone off. My best friend's ringtone, "Wake me up before you go-go," relentlessly played, forcing me to get out of the comfy bed and answer.

"Hey! How'd it go with your dad?" Devon's enthusiasm grated on my sour nerves.

"I don't wanna talk about it." I crawled back in bed with the phone.

"Are you at home? I'll bring a veggie pizza."

My weakness. My friend knew me well. "Okay."

"I'll be there in about a half hour."

"Thanks, Dev."

I WOKE TO the sound of someone rustling in the kitchen and the smell of pizza. Devon had a key to my place, and I had one to his. Following the aroma, I went into the kitchen and saw the pizza box on the counter, and Devon taking the rest of our feast out of a bag. "Got your favorite pizza, Caesar salad, and soda."

"You're a lifesaver, Dev."

He eyed me and then waved me off. "Go sit on the couch. I got this." Within seconds, Devon put plates full of salad and pizza on the small coffee table, along with two cans of soda, and a bottle of painkillers.

"You're gonna make an excellent housewife someday." I couldn't resist messing with him.

"Shut up and eat your pizza."

I turned the TV on for background noise as the two of us ate.

"How are the ribs?"

"Better."

"I'd have gone out with you last night, Os. I'd have had your back, you know."

"I know. But I figured you and Stone would be hanging out. It's the weekend." In all the years I'd known Devon, we'd been inseparable. Adjusting to him being with Stone was more difficult than I'd thought it would be. Devon must have felt equally excluded when Carrie and I were together. He never mentioned it, though.

"He's flying in tomorrow." He bit into another piece of pizza.

"How are things going between you guys?"

"Our schedules still suck, but...he wants to try anal. Like, this weekend." That had been another big issue between Devon and him, one I thought they'd remedied.

"He wants to bottom?"

"No, I do, silly. But he's not opposed to trying anything, really."

Dev loved bottoming, but my bestie clearly hadn't pushed his boyfriend. Whereas, after having one go at bottoming, I was ready to be a lap slut. Dev must have been using his vibrator left and right to scratch that itch.

"That's a good thing, right?"

"I'm a little nervous, Os. What if he doesn't like it?" He pushed his pizza away and collapsed into the sofa. "Ugh. Being with him is more work than I ever thought it would be. I'm like this insecure person around him. It's not me, and I hate it."

"You said he likes giving you head, and as far as I'm concerned, that's a good indication that he's gonna love being inside you." I bumped his shoulder. "It's all warm and cozy up in there. I can't imagine anyone not loving being that close to you." I winked. Yeah, there were feels between us.

"You're right." Dev rested his hand on my thigh. "I shouldn't be so worried. I'll just wear those thigh-high boots he loves and a miniskirt, and it'll drive him crazy." Devon sat a little taller.

"There ya go." I took another bite of the pizza, enjoying the greasy goodness.

"Wanna talk about what happened with your dad?"

My turn to go all emo. "He was there, Dev." I slumped into the sofa. "Trent was in my dad's office while he was chewing me out." Freaking embarrassing.

Devon covered his mouth. "Oh my God. Why is he in Las Vegas? What did he say when he saw you?"

"Dad said he's considering Trent for a junior partnership position and had him transfer while another attorney is out on maternity leave. He didn't recognize me, or at least he didn't let on that he did."

"Well, you *were* in full drag, and you looked drop-dead gorgeous, nothing like your normal un-fabulous garb." He grinned.

"Shut up."

"Seriously. You were unrecognizable," he consoled. "I got pictures to prove it. Charlie had no idea it was you when I showed him." Charlie was Devon's boss, and I'd known him since I was fifteen, a year less than I'd known Devon.

"It still stings."

"Poor baby," Devon said, rubbing my arm. "What are you going to do?"

"Nothing." I grabbed the painkillers and took two of them, washing them down with soda.

"Can I be honest?"

"I'd hope so."

"Promise not to get all testy?"

I shrugged.

"You got your undergrad in biology and applied to UC Davis for veterinary medicine. You want to be a veterinarian. But it all changed after you got engaged to the Beast. She got in your head."

"She wasn't that bad."

Carrie had been, though. I was just too stupid and in love to notice the way I'd let her take control of my life. When I told her about UC Davis, she protested, saying she needed to stay by her family. She also liked the idea of me being an attorney, not a vet. The battle compounded when my father pressured me to apply to law school. He preferred I go to an Ivy League, in particular, Stanford, where he'd gone. My fiancée wasn't having that either. I compromised. I chose UNLV law school, and within my first month, she'd broken off the engagement.

"Os, she saw us dancing together—not even that dirty dancing thing we used to do—and it freaked her out so much she broke up with you. What was it she said? Oh yeah, I remember. She said she thought you'd rather suck dick than be with her, and she couldn't handle it."

"She didn't say it like that." The fight echoed in my head, and her words had been permanently burned into my heart. I'd been honest with her from the first date. I told her I was bi. She'd even seen Dev and me dancing on several occasions. No matter how many times I assured her, she saw Devon and every male friend I had as a threat.

"You deserve so much better. And I don't mean that lawyer guy, either."

"You're right."

"I know."

We spent the rest of the afternoon watching Netflix. I napped on and off, waking up in the late evening to the sound of Devon in the kitchen talking.

"I'm thinking about it still," Devon said, sounding strained. "No, I can't come to LA this week. Charlie got three cars yesterday, and I have to be here to help him." Devon chuckled. "You're so cute when you beg." A long exasperated sigh. "No chance you could fly up here this week—just for, like, a day or something? I bet I can get a day off." Silence. "No, no. I understand. So maybe the following week? If we have all the parts in, I should be able to get the majority of work on the cars done." More silence. "Um, I can't right now. I'm with Os...yeah we might... I'll call you when I get home, okay? Bye, babe." Another sigh as he came back into the living room looking depressed as all hell.

I sat up, noticing how my ribs felt. Better. Not great but much better. "Everything okay?"

"It's Stone. He's working on a new album with the band, and we can't work out a schedule where I can see him." He flopped down next to me on the sofa. "He said to say hi, by the way." Devon pushed a loose lock of hair behind his ear. "He wants me to move to LA, like, temporarily, while he's working on the album. But I can't, Os. Charlie needs me."

The heartbreak in Devon's voice pierced me. I put my arm around my friend and kissed his cheek. "Is he still coming to Vegas tomorrow?"

"Yeah, but it's a quick visit." Devon twisted his lips. "This feels impossible, Os. I know once they're done with the album, they'll tour, and I won't get to see him because he'll be traipsing all over the world. What kind of relationship is that? Not to mention the media attention." He tossed up his hands. "I'm getting hounded at work. I knew Stone had a lot of fans. I just didn't think they'd be lurking around staring at me like I was some zoo animal. They follow me and follow us around whenever we go out." His voice got louder. "After what happened with Jerry, I—I don't know if I can keep doing this."

"At least he's back in prison."

When Devon was fourteen, his mom broke up with Jerry after discovering he'd been abusing her son. As soon as he was released in November, he hunted Devon down and threatened him at gunpoint. Stone had been there, and witnessed Devon kick the crap out of Jerry.

"He stalked me, threated my life and Stone's, and all he got was three years. It's not fair."

I agreed.

Jerry had taken a plea bargain for aggravated stalking and violating a protective order, and because it was a hate crime, the court treated it as a category B felony, which meant instead of a one year sentence, he got a three-year sentence. I may have been failing law school, but I wasn't ignorant of the criminal justice system.

"What am I going to do?"

"You're going to find a compromise. You're going to talk to him and work this out because you love him. But you're going to do this all later because you know what you need right now?"

He gave me a side-glance, heartbreak and frustration written all over his face. "What's that?"

"Girls Night Out."

"You're in no shape to for that." He tried to dismiss it, but a little sparkle in his eyes told me I was right. Devon was in the dumps, and as BFF, it was my duty to cheer him up. This was the best way I knew how. He'd have done the same for me.

"Screw it. Come on. I never got to try out that other outfit you wanted me to wear in LA." I stood and tried to pull him up from the couch by his arm.

He groaned. "You don't really like dressing as a woman, Os. It's okay. Maybe it's time to stop, you know?"

Oh, hell to the no. Devon was in full defeat mode. This was as bad as when his last boyfriend dumped him.

"Not true, my friend. I actually like looking beautiful. And I'll let you in on a little secret. I bought several pairs of silk undies from Etsy that I love."

"You bought them. For yourself. Without me?" Devon had always purchased the clothes, underwear, shoes, and all. He liked dressing me up, and I liked him dressing me. "And you don't wear a gaff?"

"They got a little pouch for my junk, and I only wear a dress with you, so I don't have to worry about a bulge."

"I think I'm impressed."

"Whattaya say?" I smiled, grabbing his other arm and finally moving him off the couch.

"It'd be a shame to keep that outfit I bought you in the closet." He pursed his lips as if he was contemplating going out. "Fine." An eye roll and a big dimpled smile followed. "But just 'cause the outfits I have in mind for you and me are super sexy."

I laughed. "Naturally."

Devon had everything at his house, so we went over there to get ready. I forgot my colored contacts, but it didn't matter. As it was, it took us a little over an hour to get the makeup and hair done.

"Okay, here's your outfit." Devon went into his closet and produced a black denim kilt that was pleated, a far cry from the traditional tartan. No tucking required.

"You got me a kilt? Dev! I love it!"

"It's not the usual fem thing, but I thought you'd appreciate it."

"Seriously, I love it!" I put it on and fastened the buckles on the top. "I should've gotten one of these sooner."

"Are you gonna go all *Braveheart* under there?" he asked as he handed me a skintight black top and a pair of knee-high Gothic boots with buckles and studs. The clothes were masculine, but paired with the black wig and makeup the ensemble took an androgynous turn.

"I got Irish blood in me, not Scottish, remember? And hell, yeah." I grinned and put the boots and shirt on. I liked this look—the unisex style felt comfortable. And it was definitely easier than all the primping and preening and squishing needed with the last outfit.

Devon spun around, showing off his tight dress with a decadent plunging neckline. Amazing how a little prosthetics and makeup gave him perfect cleavage. "Well, what do you think?"

"Super sexy, Dev."

"Too bad Stone's not here to see it." He frowned.

"I'll send him a picture."

Devon brightened and handed me his phone. "Wait, let me get into place." He pushed his boobs together and then studied the room for the best lighting.

"Total. Diva."

"You know it," he said as he sashayed over to the brick wall that divided the living room from the bedroom. After a few pictures—like, ten, because Devon was a picky diva—he sent one to Stone. And got an immediate response.

"He said I look so hot, he might take the last flight out to Vegas tonight." Devon practically glowed, and in turn, I felt happy for him. He jumped up and down a few times in his high-heeled boots, and the sight was so hilarious I couldn't help smiling.

"We still going out?"

"Heck yeah. After all that work, you think I'mma sit around the house and wait? Nope. Let's go!" Devon's mood had improved, and I was more than happy to ride the high with him. It was going to be fun, just like the old days before ex-fiancées and boyfriends and hot lawyers with penetrating blue eyes.

# Chapter Nine

TRENTON

I managed to find something suitable to wear in my unpacked belongings and met Georgia at the club. I thought the place would be more BDSM friendly—her typical venue. But I was mistaken. A jazz band played on one floor, a rock band on another, and on the level where we were drinking, a DJ had the crowd dancing. The upbeat location did little to improve my somber mood. I was miles away from LA, my home, the ocean, the things and people I took for granted.

"Why do you always look like someone ran over your puppy every time I see you?" Georgia asked before slamming back a shot named Wet Pussy. Needless to say, that was one drink I passed on.

"Just adjusting to the move."

"You're missing LA already? That was fast."

"You of all people should know how much I never wanted to live here again."

"Umm-hmm. Too cold. Too dry. And too far away from the ocean. I remember."

All of it was true. I'd grown up in a suburb of Boston, close to the ocean, until fifth grade when we moved to Vegas. Another reason why I'd done my undergrad and grad work in the oceanside college town. I loved Boston proper, but the winters were too brutal, colder and damper than Vegas. Wanting to stay close to the ocean without the blistering cold, I set my sights on the California coast and a career in entertainment law. I missed my family, and that was about the only thing I missed about Vegas.

"Exactly." I nursed my beer and scanned the throng of dancing bodies. "Is it just me or does everyone look so much younger these days?"

Georgia cackled. "Old man, you don't look a day over thirty-five." She elbowed me. "Seriously, you look good. You could still get yourself a quality piece tonight."

I shrugged.

"What about the hottie you met in LA?" she asked as she stared out into the dancing crowd, fixated.

"He never texted me."

"So what if I told you I think said hottie is here in Vegas? In this very club?"

My pulse spiked. I cursed the unexpected reaction. What the fuck? It wasn't as if I knew him. It wasn't as if he wanted to talk to me.

I followed Georgia's gaze and saw Sin dancing with Stone Manson's boyfriend, Devon, whom I recognized from photos. Hips swaying, laughing, arms circling each other only to pull away and twirl again. The two of them appeared to be having a good time all by themselves.

"I don't think I should bother them."

Georgia eyed me.

"If he wanted to hook up again, he would've texted." I turned around and finished off my beer in one long gulp. Fuck. He was here. Dancing a few feet away. Relief lessened the rejection. I'd thought Oisin and Sin were the same person, but the way Sin gracefully swayed and moved to the beat gave no sign of injury. "I gotta hit the can. I'll be back."

I pushed my way past the bar. My stomach twisted and turned, while my mind kept the Sin and Trent porno playing. Frustrated, I punched the door open to the restroom nearly hitting a guy in the face.

"Watch what you're doing, asshole." The guy had about twenty more pounds of muscle on him than I had.

"Fuck you." Not one of my brighter moments. Before I could set one foot inside the bathroom, the guy picked me up by my shirt and slammed me into the wall.

"Mind your fucking manners."

"Eat shit."

Boy, I was in a mood. I didn't even see the fist coming. Pain radiated across my cheek, rattling my skull. Well, at least now the external damage would match the way I felt internally. I covered my face, hoping to stave off another blow, but a couple of his buddies grabbed his arms before he could strike again.

"Let's go, man. He's not worth it." The bulky trio exited the bathroom, leaving me to do my business and take inventory of the damage. It'd bruise for sure, right along my jaw. I was fortunate he hadn't knocked out any teeth. I washed the blood off my face, but a stubborn cut refused to stop bleeding. Pressing a paper towel to my jaw, I went back to the bar.

Georgia frowned when she saw me. "You didn't."

"I did."

Georgia shook her head and stifled a laugh. "You've got to come to my dungeon soon. We'll work that aggression right out." Subbing was an invaluable tool in learning how to Dom, but otherwise, not my thing.

"I think I should le—" Fuck. Sin was right next to me, waiting to capture the bartender's attention. He hadn't noticed me, not yet.

"Trent?" he asked, his mouth open in pure shock. I bet he paled. It was hard to tell with the colored lights. No barbell in his lip. Bummer.

"Sin. Good to see you again."

"You too." His smile was genuine but fleeting. "I'm sorry I haven't texted. I—my life got a little complicated after we hooked up."

"Boyfriend?" *None of my freaking business.*

He shook his head. "No, nothing that simple."

I couldn't place it, but something about him looked different. More than just the outfit or the way he'd styled his wig. Was it the eye makeup? "Want to talk about it?"

He bit his lip and looked away. Following his line of sight, I saw Devon approaching. "Maybe another time?"

Devon was all kinds of woman and a bright smile. He said, "Isn't this the guy who works for—" before Sin nudged him. There was no reason Devon should recognize me, but clearly, he did. I filed that information away for later.

"Trent, this is Devon. Devon, this is Trent and his friend, Georgia."

"Sin can't stop talking about you." Devon shook a thumb at his friend. Sin brought his hand to his forehead, shielding his eyes, embarrassed.

"Oh really?" I drew the word out, satisfied and smug. My heart thumped, spiking to a new level of elation. No one should have this effect on me, especially someone I'd only known for one night.

"Yup. Isn't that right, Sin?"

"You'll have to excuse my friend," Sin said. "He's had a bit too much fun for the evening."

Devon put a hand to his chest, feigning offense. "Hardly. I think it's just starting, actually." He waved his hand at the bartender, immediately getting his attention, and ordered a couple drinks.

"Love your dress, Devon." Georgia's southern charm whipped loose in a sly smile. "That kilt is hot, Sin. And just so the playing field is clear, Trent has mentioned you quite a few times." She could've humiliated me worse. Frankly, I was surprised she hadn't.

The drinks arrived, and Devon handed a shot to Sin and sipped his, which suspiciously looked like the Wet Pussy Georgia slammed back moments ago.

"Devon, why don't you and I give these two some space, hmm?" Georgia asked.

A brilliant one-dimple smile spread across Devon's face, lighting it up. "I think that's a fantastic idea. Wanna dance?"

"Perfect." Georgia turned to me and winked. "I won't wait up for you."

Sin looked up at the ceiling, maybe silently praying to a higher power, or cursing his friend for leaving.

Insecurity was foreign to me, yet having been rejected by Sin, I began to overthink what I should say or do now that we were alone. I went with the most obvious choice.

"Dance with me," I said, more like an order than a request.

He bit his lip—exactly what I wanted to do—and reached for my hand.

I laced my fingers with his, finding the contact replaced my self-doubt with an entirely different emotion.

The music pulsed. The strobe lights flashed. Sin rocked his hips, swaying his booty to the beat. When I finally tore my gaze away from him, he flashed a self-satisfied grin. Busted. Still, no one swirled their body like that unless they wanted to be watched.

"Tell me one thing—what's under that kilt?"

A smile broke out across his face. "Nothing," he replied as he rocked his body side to side with the music. "Absolutely nothing."

It may have been better not to know. All I could think of was taking him into the bathroom and lifting that kilt up and fucking him senseless. I settled for placing a hand on his hip, the fabric damp with sweat. He danced closer until there was only a breath between us. Spinning around so his back was against my chest, he dropped it low, sticking that fine booty out. I enjoyed the view, continuing to bounce behind him to the rhythm. He stood up, not so gracefully, and clung on to my arm, laughing, tossing his head back, his smile wide and his eyes closed. That was a beautiful sight. I wished the music wasn't so loud so I could hear the sound of his laughter.

We continued dancing through a few more songs, boldly touching, grinding, and bumping to the beat, until I'd had about all I could take. I pulled him close and kissed his neck, breathing in his sweat and tasting its salty flavor. He angled his head, granting me better access, and I kissed and licked my way up to his jaw and to his lips where I claimed him, parting his lips with my tongue. Diving in, I fused our mouths, relishing the feel of our tongues lapping and twining sloppily. It was fucking dirty, dry humping on the dance floor. I needed to feel his flesh under me, touch those beautiful tattoos, play with his piercings.

"Come home with me."

He placed a hand on my chest, gently pushing us apart. Tension creased his forehead, and he looked pained. It was certainly not the expression I'd hoped to see. "I-I should go find Devon. It's getting late."

I'd been foolish. Sin had rejected me before and nothing had changed. I should let him go, but I'd grown possessive. He occupied a place in me that had been a dark void before, filling it with his light and his sweetness. "I didn't mean to make it hard on you, Sin. I understand. Like you said, whatever's going on with you is complicated. I live in Vegas now, so if you do change your mind, call me."

I'd been kissed goodbye before, bittersweet and desperate, and that was precisely the kiss Sin gave me. He'd never call. I closed my eyes and froze this moment in my mind, capturing the softness of his lips, the taste of his sweat, the scent of his cologne, the feel of him in my arms. The kiss ended all too soon. He removed his hands from my neck, severing the connection we'd made and leaving me unmoored.

"Let's go find your friend," I said, trying to avoid the heartache swelling inside. All the years I'd been with Nic, I'd never experienced this overwhelming need to be with him, not like I did with Sin. It consumed me. It could ruin me. I swallowed it down and reached for Sin's hand, letting him lead.

We searched the crowd and found Devon and Georgia dancing and laughing in the middle of the dance floor. They waved us over. Sin leaned into Devon and said something to which Devon nodded.

"Looks like we're heading out," Devon shouted above the music. "We'll chat soon." He touched Georgia's arm.

"You got it, sugar," she replied. She was definitely up to no good, judging by her sly side grin.

Sin turned to me and kissed my cheek. "Thanks for a fun night." With a small wave, he and Devon left, and I watched until I could no longer see them. *Pathetic. Disappointed. Rejected.*

I drew my hand to where Sin's lips had touched my cheek.

"You got it bad for that one," Georgia chaffed.

"I do. I don't know why, but I do." Denying my attraction was pointless.

"I know why." Georgia's all too familiar smug grin appeared.

"Okay, I'll bite. Why?"

"You're used to getting your way, and that pretty young thing left you high and dry after your first hookup, and he just did it again."

"That's not..." It was partly true, but there was so much more. I exhaled and took a look around at the dancing bodies. Without Sin there, the club no longer excited me. "Think I'm going to call it a night."

"All right, old man. You do that. I'm gonna stick around."

We hugged our goodbyes, and I left the *thumpa thumpa* behind. A blast of cold wind assaulted me as I stepped into the late night air, sliding into the crevices of my coat and pointing out the damp parts of my clothing. What I wouldn't give to be back in Cali under her sunshine.

But then there would be no Sin.

I chided myself because the mere thought was pathetic. I had no time for a relationship. No time to be playing the "oh, I hope he likes me" game. But my stupid body seemed to have its own agenda. I'd futilely tried to push thoughts of him out of my mind, but he left me curious. Left me wanting more. Georgia was right; I always got what I put my mind to. Except Sin. I hadn't gotten him...yet.

But I would.

# Chapter Ten

TRENTON

At Sunday brunch with my family I'd been able to keep my mind off the sting of Sin's rejection until my mother mentioned my single status. Melissa proudly announced she'd set me up on a blind date, and despite Mere and me badgering her for details about my mystery man, Melissa remained tight-lipped. My mother chimed in, saying she feared I was missing out on the things that really mattered in life by working so much. I did, too. I'd avoided work all weekend for that reason, and as punishment, I'd spent the entire morning catching up.

Harrison's number flashed on my phone. Great. More pressure for a Monday morning.

"Fisher," his grumbly bass greeted me. "How are things going? Settling into Vegas okay? Everyone in the office behaving?"

"Yes, everyone is professional."

"Have you set up a time to meet with Oisin?"

"We tentatively scheduled Wednesday." My phone chirped. A text message with a phone number appeared.

"There's his number so you can confirm," Harrison said. "He'll be expecting your call." Given our last conversation, I doubted Oisin would return any communication I offered, but Harrison had now put it upon me to try.

I heard the squeak of his chair and papers being shuffled in the background. Silence was uncommon for Harrison, which meant he was weighing his next words.

"I can't tell you how much Angel and I appreciate your help. I've been at a loss with him. My first son, Dan, was so strong-willed. He knew what he wanted and just went for it. I thought he'd help out his little brother, but he's touring the world with a theater company and..." For Harrison to be searching for words, something he never did, proved the situation with Oisin was difficult. "Do you know why I chose you, Fisher, aside from your qualifications?"

"No, sir."

"Oisin is struggling. I've seen him with men and women, and frankly, I don't understand or have the slightest idea how a person can be like that. Dan always liked men. There was never a question. But Oisin? I thought he was straight until he met Devon. Then he started dressing in women's clothing like Devon, and then he dated Devon." He let out a puff of air. "I was okay with all of that. Admittedly, it was an adjustment, a shock, but he seemed happy and that was what ultimately mattered. What I'm not okay with is this dark streak I've seen in my son lately. It's like he's half there. I know, I know. I've been away in LA most of the time, but Angel keeps tabs on her boy—he is her favorite—and she's worried, too. And I'm not sure if it's him questioning his sexuality, or perhaps how he identifies that has him in such a state. Or if it's heartbreak now that Devon is with that heavy metal singer, or-or...something else."

"Devon Thomson? Stone Manson's boyfriend?" I cringed. Being identified as so-and-so's boyfriend belittled Devon's individuality, but I had to be certain we were talking about the same Devon Thomson.

"Yes. Do you know him?"

"No, I..." Oisin was friends with Devon. Oisin dated Devon. Last time I'd met Sin, he'd been with Devon. I mentally retraced Saturday night and remembered something was different about him...his eyes. They were brown when I'd met him in Los Angeles but much a lighter color, possibly hazel, at the club Saturday...similar to Oisin's.

And Oisin's voice.

*Oh God. Oh no.* I was so fucked. Had I slept with my boss's son?

I scrubbed a hand down my face. "And how does that make me qualified?" I did my best to harness my shock at what Harrison had alluded; he'd chosen me because I was gay. Then again, Harrison was a smart guy. By asking me to help his son, he'd opened himself and his company up for a harassment lawsuit, something only a desperate man would do.

"He and I fight. I can't get through to him. He's been screwing up since Carrie called off their engagement last September. I think he's drinking too much, possibly using drugs. I'm worried he's self-destructing, and Angel and I are stuck on the sidelines. Keep this between us, Fisher. My wife and I are in legal separation, and I know that is hurting him. I'm hoping he confides in you. Maybe he'll listen to you and get help before something serious happens. You have your life together even after separating from your partner, and I thought you might offer some understanding, like a big brother. Maybe clear up any confusion he has about sexual identity. I won't pry and ask what the two of you discuss, but if you see any signs that he's...unstable...please let me know."

The man I had aspired to be like, whom I admired for his tough business acumen and intelligence, and whose exterior persona had always been professional and approachable, had crumbled. The unsteadiness in his demeanor as he pled for me to help his son was unexpected and unlike anything I'd ever heard from him.

I remained uncertain as to how much I could actually assist in this situation. Oisin was a grown man, capable of making his own decisions, and for whom attending mentoring with me was not a priority.

But we had screwed each other senseless.

"I will," I promised.

Harrison thanked me and hung up.

*This is not happening.* I buried my face in my hands and took a deep breath. I had to leave to make it to the blind date. It'd be rude to cancel—rude to my sister. She meant well. Better to just rip the Band-Aid off and go to lunch. Not that I was in the mood to eat after that conversation.

The brisk February air made the short walk to the upscale restaurant unpleasant. Plants and traditional Thai-inspired decorations of Buddha and elephants adorned the entrance, while a small partition dissected the entrance from the main dining area.

"Lunch for one?" the hostess asked, picking up a menu.

"I'm meeting someone." Feeling ridiculous and silently cursing my sister, I added, "Under the reservation of gingerbread man."

She broadened her smile. "Oh, yes. He's here. Follow me." She led me into the main dining area, and I knew as soon as we turned the corner I was well and utterly fucked. Oisin Harrison was sitting in a booth, and we were heading right toward him.

# Chapter Eleven

OISIN

I stared at the menu for the hundredth time, not seeing a thing on it. I'd get pad Thai. I always got pad Thai; it was my favorite. I'd have cancelled the date if the man wasn't Melissa's brother. Poor guy. Thoughts of Trent kept creeping into my head like a habit I couldn't shake. Why did he have to be at that club Saturday night, enticing me, tempting me by smelling as good as he did and looking all sexy in those tight pants? Alcohol had numbed the pain in my ribs and loosened up my inhibitions, hence the tonsil hockey session and the bump and grind on the dance floor. His mouth was magic. And I loved his teeth—a quirky thing—but he had these even front teeth and kinda pointy canines that felt amazing on my tongue...and when he bit my neck. A little Dracula-like without the overkill.

Devon texted, asking if my date had arrived. I had the phone in my hand, ready to type back a sarcastic comment about how rude it'd be to text if the guy was here, when Trent came around the corner with the hostess. Trent. In a suit. Hot in all kinds of ways. Then again, the guy could be wearing footed pajamas and I'd still find him irresistible. The navy fabric hugged him in all the right places, showcasing his lean physique. His short hair was styled back with a little lift, adding to his professional appearance. He knew how to dress to impress; we're talking London Fashion Week with all the goods and no tweed.

Every time I saw him, he stole my breath. Completely unfair. He had to be here on his lunch break. The firm was within walking distance. This was just a coincidence—*uh-oh.*

"Here you go, sir," the hostess said as she sat Trent at my table. I stared. Blatantly. I got sucked in, remembering the heat in his eyes, the way his lips felt all over my body, the way he marked me with his teeth, the way we fit together dancing, and in bed.

He slid into the seat across from mine. "I didn't realize you knew my sister." He gave no indication that learning I was his blind date bothered him. He seemed calm, his voice smooth and without the slightest bit of tension.

"I didn't realize she was your sister," I mumbled, looking away, trying not to get lost in everything Trent. I silenced my phone and set it face down on the table.

"She mentioned you—well, my blind date—volunteered at her clinic."

I shifted uncomfortably and rolled up my sleeves, basically fidgeting. "I like working with animals." I shrugged. "I'd hoped to go into veterinary medicine."

Trent eyed my forearm. The tattoos were the one thing I hadn't covered that night we'd been together. Maybe I should confess, tell him we'd already slept together and move on. Nothing more would or could happen anyway, so it wasn't like I was jeopardizing anything by offering the truth.

"If you wanted to be a veterinarian, why study law?" he asked, picking up the menu and glancing it over.

"I fell in love, and she wanted to stay close to Vegas."

He focused on my face again, my lips specifically. I had the barbell in, the one he'd liked against his flesh when I had his dick in my mouth. "That doesn't answer my question," he replied, meeting my eyes.

We were dodging the enormous issue of him working for my father—regardless if he'd recognized Sin's tattoos—and that this date would go nowhere. Maybe he'd already dismissed any chance of this being an actual date. Maybe he was upset to learn his date was with me because he was hoping for someone to actually be with. That thought made me jealous.

"Reno is the only school with a degree in veterinary medicine. Carrie, my ex, had all her family close to Las Vegas and wanted us to stay close to them."

"I see." He returned to studying the menu.

The waitress approached and asked if we were ready to order. We both agreed. I got pad Thai and Trent got yellow curry, mild spice.

"You're at a Thai restaurant and you ask for mild spice?" The idea appalled me. Thai food was supposed to be flammable. The hotter, the better.

"It's not a pretty picture if I indulge in spicy food."

My mind raced back to how touchy he was about being thirty, and I couldn't help myself. "Yes, I imagine someone of your age would have issues with digestion."

He threw his napkin in my face. "I'm not that old." A few lines creased the corners of his eyes as he laughed. This was a new side of Trent, a playful side I hadn't seen, and it made me eager to learn more about him, especially if I got to see that smile again.

"Of course not, grandpa." I tossed the napkin back at him. "Should I order a side of mashed potatoes? I know your dentures don't hold up well." I grinned.

"You deserve a spanking, boy." He lowered his voice and shot me a look that was deadly serious.

My knees weakened with the image he presented, and God help me, my cock jumped. Regardless, he was not getting the upper hand. "There's nothing I'd like more than a good spanking, Sir," I countered, meeting his intense gaze.

Without flinching he said, "That can be arranged." Trent flashed a wicked smirk. His eyes were alight with mischief and setting a charge in my now less-roomy pants. Thank God they were stretchy.

Suddenly thirsty, I took a long drink of my water.

"So you gave up the career you wanted for the person you loved, and now, according to your dad, you're failing law school to the point he wants me to mentor you." Apparently he was going to ignore that little D/s exchange.

"I'm sorry about that. My dad, that is. Not about failing. I think I'm a lost cause at this point." If I did nothing but study I could probably pull my grades up, but I had no motivation. Well, Trent might be motivation. Who was I kidding? He'd be more a distraction. He *was* a distraction.

"We can't control our parents," he dismissed. Thankfully, he left my grades alone. "How are you feeling, by the way? Still sore?"

"Not really. Tender, but nothing like Saturday." I sighed. Flirting and talking with Trent and not telling him who I was seemed dishonest, and it wasn't sitting well. I had to expose the five hundred ton elephant sitting on the table before it crushed me. "Um, there's something I need to tell you."

He pointed to the tattoo on my arm, the one with the writing—The Wounds are Where the Light Gets In. "I know, Oisin. I figured it out. It's okay."

"I'm sorry. I had no idea who you were when we hooked up in Hollywood. And Saturday, I just thought...I don't know...it was nice just to dance with you."

What the hell was that look on his face? Pity? Longing?

"We can't change what happened."

This was the part where he'd boot me. Where he'd say it was a mistake, and we shouldn't see each other again, regardless of how much we might want to. I subscribed to that sentiment; it just sucked. Trent was a good lover, and one I wanted to ride again. Not to mention, he was my first experience with anal sex. Toys weren't the same.

"Would you want to?" I blurted.

"No." He didn't hesitate. "I liked being with you, Oisin, and I was looking forward to seeing you again."

"I was too." I wish I could've held back the smile, but his confession had made it impossible for me to be anything but happy.

Our food arrived. Trent took a tentative bite and fanned his mouth. "Hot, oh..." He swallowed and drank some water. Watching him morph from all seriousness to a guy whose food got the best of him was adorable.

"So what do we do?" I asked and reluctantly ate some noodles. The inevitable would happen. We couldn't see each other again. It'd screw up my relationship with my father and put my trust fund and future at stake. And Trent wouldn't risk upsetting his boss and his career.

"Well, I'll continue to mentor you like Harrison wants."

My mind went in the gutter, to places where he mentored me by spanking, choking, biting, and screwing me in his office. "I don't think I'd be able to concentrate much." I frowned. "Besides, I'm sure you'll have to report all our little interactions to my father, and that puts you in a crappy place." I pushed my food aside.

Sitting back, he said, "Harrison is more concerned about your welfare than what's going on with law school. He thinks you're partying too much, possibly doing drugs."

"I'm not. Well, the partying maybe. The drugs—I've taken them once or twice, but I'm not addicted. My father thinks I'm a failure. He has for a while. I didn't go to the law school he wanted. I didn't marry the woman I was supposed to. He doesn't understand why I dress in drag. He doesn't understand what being bisexual means. And before you say it, I know he tries. He's just never around and when he is, he ends up yelling at me, or getting frustrated."

Rubbing his bottom lip, Trent seemed to be pondering my words. "I don't want to be in the middle of this, and if it was anyone but you, Oisin, I wouldn't." He paused and let out a breath. "I promise anything you say to me I will not repeat to your father or anyone else. It stays between us."

"So you want us to be what? Like, friends?"

"I'm not sure how I could be just friends with you," he stated. "I can't seem to forget you or the way you looked that night we were together. I can't seem to forget the way you smelled, tasted, or felt. And I don't want to forget it, either. I want you in my arms again. I want to be able to kiss you, dance with you, be naked with you again."

Not once did he look away. He practically dared me to jump his bones right here in the restaurant. Heat crept all over my body, and of course my dick wanted in on that action. "Are you always so forward?" I'd always been the pursuer in my hookups. I'd never had anyone flat-out tell me they wanted me, and I was just the type to go belly-up for the attention.

"When I want something, I usually get it."

"Oh, do you? And what happens when your boss finds out you've been screwing his son? Or that instead of babysitting him, you broke his heart and left him worse than before?" I tossed my napkin on the table. "I can't do this. I'm okay with fucking up my life, but I'm not going to drag you into it. I'll tell Dad to find someone else to mentor me." I stood and walked away, getting only a few feet before Trent grabbed my wrist.

"Oisin, wait." He pulled me around to face him.

"It's not going to work, Trent. Not for your career. Not for my sanity. Dad will take away my trust fund if he finds out, and I've no idea what he could do to you, legally. But with the kind of man he is, he'd probably open a special office in Alaska and transfer you to it. Whatever is going on between us, it's not worth all that, is it?" My insides were screaming, *please say YES!*

Trent twined his fingers with mine, and I died just a little inside. It was like the support I'd been looking for was right there, and if the world fell apart, it wouldn't matter because he'd be beside me and we'd have each other. My instincts, based upon my past choices, were terrible. My heart was imagining things that weren't there; I was sure of it.

He took a step closer. "You feel it, too. I can see it in your eyes, Oisin. You want me."

And there went my knees, my legs turning into wet noodles. Useless.

"What happens when you get what you want and leave? Goal attained. Mission completed, and on to the next?" My voice wavered, not half as strong as I'd hoped.

He looked down to where our hands were joined. Letting go, he wrapped his hand around the nape of my neck, bringing our bodies together and our faces inches apart. "I'm not going to beg or plead. I will ask you once and only once. Give us a chance. I don't know much about you, and you know even less about me. Part of my job is to be with you, and it gives us the perfect excuse to get to know each other. I'm asking you to take advantage of it. See where this goes. We don't have to do anything you don't want to do." He carded his fingers through my hair, and I stifled a groan, silently cursing him for feeling so darn good. "When I saw you sitting at the table, I intended to ignore what happened between us because, like you said, the risks are high. But I didn't get where I am today without taking risks, and when I see something worth taking a chance on, I go for it."

No one had ever taken such a huge risk on me. No one. Including myself. The air left my lungs. I could barely think, let alone talk.

"We have time," he continued. "Let's use it. We can decide later what to do."

"Yes." A single word, and relief flooded me, tricking me into thinking things would go well, that Trent and I might have a happily ever after—because, hello, hopeless romantic here.

Truthfully, it was probably just a matter of time before things went tits up.

# Chapter Twelve

Trenton

When I returned to my office, Jana had left a stack of phone messages on my desk with the corresponding files—a sight befitting of Monday since clients had all weekend to drum up urgent matters. I'd get to them later. The personal phone call I had to make surpassed all my clients' issues. I closed my office door and phoned my sister.

"How'd it go?" Melissa asked.

"Meh, it was okay."

"You're a terrible liar. Are you sure you're a lawyer?"

"You got me, Sis. I'm actually a proctologist."

"So you liked him then?" she asked, not fazed by my comment.

"I did. He's a very likable person." Oisin and I had agreed to keep whatever was going on between us a secret. Melissa would be the exception. "He's my boss's son."

"What?" Her voice went shrill. "Oisin never mentioned anything about his father being a lawyer. He said his dad owned a business. Trent, I never would've set you up with him had I known." She paused, and I could picture her crinkling her nose like she always did when she was heavy in thought. "Does that mean you won't see him again?"

I rubbed my lips, pondering how much I should relay. Melissa had always been the wise one, the one I'd call when I had a problem. I'd told her I was gay before I told anyone else and she'd kept it secret until I was ready to come out. I could trust her. "You have to keep this between us, okay?"

"This sounds juicy. I pinky promise and cross my heart."

"It's about Sin—you know, the guy I met back in LA that I told you about?"

"How could I forget? I didn't think Oisin would stand a chance after the way you got all lovesick talking about Sin yesterday."

"I did not."

"Did, too. But go on. What about him?"

"Turns out Oisin and Sin are one and the same."

"Oh, Trent. Wow, that's…"

"I know."

"Wow."

"Yeah."

"Well, at least I was right—the two of you did get along. Seriously though, what are you going to do?"

"I like him, Melissa, and I can tell he likes me. But until we decide how serious we are, we're keeping it a secret. We agreed it'd be better for Harrison not to know for obvious reasons."

"That's not like you to sneak around behind your boss's back."

"I don't have an alternative. I'm not willing to let him or my job go, and I'm hoping I won't have to choose."

"I don't know whether to be happy for you or sad. It sounds like you've found something special, little brother, and it's got a huge risk tied to it. Do you think your boss would fire you if he found out?"

I snorted, remembering what Oisin said. "Well, if I have an emergency transfer to a new branch in Alaska, you'll know why. No, he can't legally fire me. He could make my life hell if he wanted, possibly ruin my career, given the firm's weight in the industry, but Harrison isn't that kind of guy. I think, at worst, he won't recommend me for junior partner."

"That partnership was your dream. It was all you talked about at Christmas." Melissa seemed stunned and rightfully so. I'd focused with laser intensity on that partnership after my breakup, and I'd been convinced Harrison would offer it to me after the holidays, which he did.

"Things change."

The emptiness of my new home reflected my career and my life. The past few nights in Vegas were lonelier than California ever had been. I thought I'd be okay with the move. That being away from everything that reminded me of Nic would heal me. But the void took residence in my heart and echoed back in every room of the firm-owned house I rented. My job was all I had, and no, that thought wasn't comfortable to snuggle up to at night. Oisin had been far warmer.

"I like this side of you. It's like the little brother I knew before he got his head up the company's ass."

"Yeah, well, don't get used to it. There's something else I wanted to talk to you about. Oisin said he wanted to be a veterinarian, and I'm assuming that's why he volunteers at your clinic."

"He does, and he's amazing with animals. But he's done more than that. He helped us establish a nonprofit charity for pet owners who couldn't afford veterinary care in addition to organizing several fundraisers. He's been a part of this clinic since he started high school."

"How come I never heard about him?"

"I've mentioned him in passing, but I'm not surprised you don't remember. You've been so wrapped up in your career, and forgive me for calling it like it is, but you pretty much shut us out. At Christmas you were on your phone almost the entire time, and that's typical of all your visits." It seemed blatant honesty was a family trait.

"I'm sorry, Mel. I should've paid more attention to you all; you're right."

"And you're right; you should've." She was quiet for a moment. "Something's changed in you. You never apologized that quickly before."

"Don't tell anyone. I can't let my reputation of being a coldhearted ass be ruined."

She chuckled. "I promise. The news of your melted heart is safe with me."

"Thank you."

"Anytime."

"Can I ask a favor?"

"You'll have to be my house slave in exchange, but sure."

"Done," I quickly replied. "Oisin mentioned going to UC Davis, where you did. Do you still have some connections back there?"

"You are so smitten with that little hottie." She had that cutesy voice that meant if I was anywhere in her presence she would've pinched my cheek.

"When he mentioned becoming a veterinarian he looked heartbroken, like his dream got crushed. I think if the door opened for him again, if I could guide him into it, he'd be happier." Opening that door seemed like a mentor-like thing to do.

"Did he tell you he got accepted into UC Davis and the veterinary medicine program? That all he has to do is say yes? I've already spoken with my former advisors and gave him a letter of recommendation. I even helped him with the application."

"No, he hasn't."

"He hasn't told me if he's going or not, but if you convince him, I'll help in any way possible. I truly believe he'd make an amazing doctor."

"Thanks, Sis."

"So, is he coming to Sunday dinner?" Melissa was well aware she was pushing her luck. "Mom would be thrilled. So will my daughter. He's amazing with her, just in case you ever thought of having any little ones."

"Goodbye, Mel."

She laughed. "Bye, Trent. And see you both Sunday."

Unfortunately, it was all too easy to imagine Oisin having dinner with my family. He already knew my sisters and my niece. Melissa said she'd known Oisin for years, since he was a kid in high school. She'd been mentoring him and thought enough of him to push him into his dream career and to set us up on a date, which meant she cared about him and could see him as part of our family. I hadn't thought her acceptance of a man I liked would mean so much, but it did. I could see a future with Oisin, and as a result, the loneliness I'd been feeling dimmed. Wednesday was two days away, but it might as well have been an eternity.

# Chapter Thirteen

OISIN

My classes yesterday had gone by as fast as two snails getting it on. Morning was no better. More like the speed of turtles clanking shells. Yup. I was measuring time in terms of animal sex. Trent was on my brain, and the anticipation of Wednesday's mentoring session had the days and hours dragging by. But it was finally here, and my mind supplied all kinds of things he could mentor me on, none of which involved case studies, contracts, or legal briefs. My fantasies had been elaborate, and if I were majoring in masturbation, I'd be getting stellar grades.

I promised Devon I'd stop by his apartment before meeting Trent at the firm.

"Thank God you're here!" he squealed as he hugged me. "I'm freaking out. Completely freaking out, and I don't know what to do." Devon looked tired, spent, and very unfashionable. His hair wasn't even styled. That could mean one of two things: he hadn't had time to change after work, or he'd spent all day worrying.

Without a word, I went into the kitchen, dove into his wine stash, and uncorked a bottle. There was no time to let it air; this was an emergency. I poured two glasses of the merlot and handed him one, which he downed in a couple inelegant gulps before handing it to me.

"More, please."

I filled the glass, gave it back, and led us to the sofa. "Talk to me, Dev. What's going on?" I made myself comfortable on the plush leather. Devon had great taste in all things, including clothes, furniture, and interior design. Neither of his parents approved of his nature, but my mom thought the world of him. When she discovered his talent for interior design, she had him stage several of her investment properties. Devon's apartment was one of them, and as payment, she let him live there rent-free.

"I think I just broke up with Stone," he said as he sat on the opposite side of the sofa.

"Oh no! Did it not go well last weekend?" Last I knew, they were going to try anal sex. If Stone didn't like it, that'd be a major hurdle for their relationship.

"What? Oh, no. That was... Let's just say the man knows how to work my body." A blush crept over Devon's cheeks. It must have been *really* good.

"Then what happened?"

He sucked on his lip, a nervous trait we had in common, and a crinkle formed between his eyebrows. "Stone got upset because he really wants me to live with him. As in move in with him. In his place. In Los Angeles. Not temporary. And then Charlie offered me his shop and..." Devon was one step away from a full-blown anxiety attack.

I looked directly into his eyes and said, "Breathe. Just breathe, okay?"

He nodded, finished off the second glass of wine, and set it on the distressed-wood coffee table, the surface of which was covered by a sheet of glass to prevent stains. The two of us couldn't have been more different when it came to decorating our homes. My apartment looked more like a tornado of books, clothes, and haphazard piles of stuff. Maybe even left over food containers. It'd been some time since I cleaned. Devon's picture-perfect apartment belonged in a trendy magazine. The architecture, inspired by the open floor plans of New York lofts, used brick, floor-to-ceiling windows, and had an exposed black ceiling. I loved the place. I'd spent more time here as an undergrad than I did at my apartment on campus.

"Or drink. Whichever works better." I shrugged and took a sip of the merlot. Not bad. "Vegas is your home, Dev, and working on cars is what you love. I can't see Stone being upset if you chose to stay. Why can't the two of you get a place to share here?" But I wasn't sure if Devon had heard a word I said, he looked so deep in thought.

"We've been dating for four months. Four months! That's not enough time to be talking about moving in with each other, let alone jumping across state borders to do it."

"What did he say when you told him that?"

"I didn't. I just sort of freaked out when he asked and said it was a crazy idea."

I set my glass down and reached out to him, taking both his hands in mine. "You love him. I know it. You know it. You'll kick yourself in the ass if you don't make this work. Talk to him, okay? Take a day and go somewhere without anyone else and just talk. You can work something out, and it'll be worth it."

With worry deep in his eyes, he said, "You sound just like your mom."

"You already talked to her?"

"Unavoidable. She stopped by with some of that veggie pasta thing I love, and I had just hung up with Stone." He tousled his hair, enhancing the chaotic mess. "You're both right, though. I should do that. It's all just moving so fast, and it's scary. I'm his first relationship with a man. What if he decides he's not into dick all of a sudden?"

"You sound like Carrie, you know that?" Bitterness filled my mouth. I never thought my best friend would question anyone who was bisexual after knowing the heartbreak I went through with my ex. It stung. "She was my first relationship with a woman, and she worried I wouldn't be into her 'all of sudden.'"

"Shit, you're right. I'm so sorry."

"Stone is bi. He's attracted to women, sure, but he's in love with *you*." I hardly believed I had to explain bisexuality to Devon. "He's never been ashamed to be with you since day one. I've seen the way he is around you, the way he looks at you, and if that isn't love, I don't know what is. Stone wouldn't ask you to live with him if he wasn't into you, all of you, dick or no dick."

"What would you do?"

I thought about it, putting Trent in the boyfriend role. If we loved each other the way Dev and Stone did, I'd do it. Then again, I'd sacrificed my dreams to be with Carrie and look where that had gotten me. Dev's dream was to own a classic and vintage car shop. Opportunities like that didn't happen every day, and he had to take it.

"Only you know what's right. But if you don't at least try to make it work, I think you'll always be wondering." I knew that was true. If I'd never tried to make it work with Carrie, I'd have regretted that decision more. I still had a chance at my dream—if I could get my courage together.

He got up and poured himself another glass of wine. "I'll call him later and have him book me on a flight to LA this weekend." Devon ran his finger along the top of the wine glass, seeming to collect his thoughts. "I'm sorry I went all Beast on you. I never thought about how you and Stone were in the same position. I never meant to hurt you."

"I know." I joined him in the kitchen and gave him a hug and kissed his cheek. "Thank you." When I let him go, I noticed the time. I had less than fifteen minutes to make it to meet Trent. "Crap, I gotta go."

"Big date?"

Damned if I could hold back a grin. "Not really, no. Maybe. I don't know." Trent never confirmed if this was a date or a mentoring session.

"Oh my gawd! You're beaming! Like, glowing. You really like this guy." Devon poked my shoulder and laughed. "I'm so happy for you. Who is he?"

"Trent." I'd talked to Devon after my lunch date with Trent and told him everything. The day after I'd slept with Trent, I'd shown Dev his photo on the company's website to explain why I wouldn't be enjoying a repeat performance with the most gracious lover I'd ever been with. That was then. Before he'd magically appeared in Las Vegas, draining my resolve.

Devon's jaw dropped. "I didn't think you had it in you to go behind your dad's back."

"He's worth it. But I don't know if tonight is a date or just some mentoring thing."

"Girl, that guy is putting his career on the line for you. It's a date, and you have to give me details later."

"I will. But I'll be late if I don't leave right now."

"Go, before your carriage turns into a pumpkin!"


MY PALMS GOT clammy on the way to the firm. The little butterflies in my stomach turned into a buzzing swarm in the elevator, and as I walked toward Trent's office, I thought my heart would leap out of my chest. This was ridiculous. I had to calm down. Taking some deep breaths, I steadied myself. Hopefully, Trent wouldn't notice the effect he had on me.

I was in deep, and I was a complete fool for him.

Trent greeted me with a wide smile that did nothing to slow my heartbeat. "Hi, come in." He motioned for me to have a seat on his sofa.

*So much for control.* I felt awkward, uncoordinated, and out of place. I had no idea what would happen, but I did have some fantasies, none of which should be acted upon in his office.

He put everything in neat piles on his desk and sat on the corner of it...like I had cooties. Or smelled funny. Or—

"Oisin?" Trent raised his eyebrows.

Crap. Was I staring? I was. Sigh. "I spent Monday and Tuesday with the tutor Dad found," I said, trying a diversion, "and honestly, I'm pretty burned out on studying, in case that's what you're planning for tonight. I could use a drink." I needed food, but my stomach was a whirlwind of winged creatures. Maybe another glass of wine would help.

"If you don't mind leaving the office, I'd like to take you to dinner. I worked straight through lunch."

"I don't mind, no." Was this was an official date? I lacked the courage to ask.

"Great. Do you like steak?"

"I'm a vegetarian, well, most of the time. I cheat sometimes but overall, yeah." And now, I was rambling.

My vegetarian status didn't seem to faze Trent. "How about Italian food?"

"I heard Panevino has a good vegetarian selection, but it has a kinda date-like atmosphere." It was pathetic, trying to get a reaction from him. But I needed to know! He typed something into his cell phone, and when he didn't respond, I figured I'd failed. Completely. I'd have to be more blunt.

Holding the phone to his ear, he said, "Yes, I'd like to make a reservation for two. Is anything available within the next hour? That would be perfect. Thank you." He tucked his phone in his pocket. "We're all set. By the time we get there, our table will be ready."

"Did you...are we..." I swallowed, trying to get the words out. "Is this a date?"

He had a mischievous gleam in his eyes. "I'd like it to be, but if you're uncomfortable with the idea, we can go someplace less 'date-like.'"

It was all I could do not to throw my arms around him and kiss him until he couldn't breathe. "I can't remember the last time I was on an actual date." Every cell in my body tingled with happiness. "Thank you."

"You're thanking me for asking you out?" He sat beside me on the sofa.

I shrugged. "Yeah, I guess I am. That's silly, huh?"

"It's incredibly sweet." Trent caressed my cheek, sending my heart into an erratic rhythm.

*Danger! Danger! Do not kiss Trent in his office!*

"As much as I love what you're doing, this probably isn't the smartest place to do it."

"You're absolutely right." He leaned forward and whispered in my ear, "We should get going." But instead of leaving, he kissed a path down my neck—my weakest spot—while cradling the back of my head, angling it for better access.

An indiscernible groan, most likely a curse of some flavor, passed my lips. I closed my eyes as he unfastened the button on my pants.

"Lower your pants. I want to feel all of you." His commanding voice had me scooting my pants lower without a second thought. He pushed me down, one hand on my stomach, the other freeing my dick and thumbing the curved bar at its tip.

"You're already hard for me." I felt his smile upon my cheek as he continued stroking my dick with lazy pumps. With my pants as low as they could go without removing my shoes, Trent slid his free hand under my ass and found the hoop in my guiche, sending a jolt along my balls and shaft.

"Oh God, that feels so good." I grabbed onto his shoulder and lifted my hips to fuck into his hand. I loved that it was him doing this to me. I loved knowing he wanted me so much he couldn't wait, that he had to have me in his office.

Every limb tightened when he breached my hole while stroking my dick. "Oh, fuck! Trent!" His hot breath fanned my neck as he kissed, nipped, and sucked those magical spots. My hips jerked involuntarily, and I was a split second away from ruining a perfectly good sweater.

"That's it, Oisin, come for me. Let everything go." He bit down on the juncture where my neck and shoulder met, causing a volcanic eruption to shoot all the way to my cheek. When I regained my senses, Trent was licking the splash of come off my face.

"You taste good." He lifted the hand that had been on my dick and was now drenched in come and brought it to my mouth. "Try it." The thick, creamy substance dripped off his hand and hit my stomach.

I'd once tasted myself as a teenager, never done it with a lover. There was a lot of come on his hand, and I wasn't sure eating it would be sexy. What if I gagged? Sure, I'd swallowed before, but in the heat of the moment, it'd been easier...and it wasn't mine.

Unsure, I went to suck his finger, and he stopped me.

"Lick, don't suck," he rumbled. That sultry, stern voice had my spent cock twitching.

Holding his gaze, I stuck my tongue out and had a taste of it—salty, sticky. The only thing that made this hot was the intent way Trent was watching me. He wet his lips. The whole thing was bizarrely perverse and had me hard again. I wanted to return the favor and drop to my knees and take him in my mouth, let him use me and fuck me until he lost control.

"So fucking hot." He captured my mouth, no doubt tasting my spunk as his tongue met mine.

I broke off our kiss, needing air. "If this is what mentoring me is like, I can't wait to see what else you've got to teach me."

"I can't wait to show you." He rubbed his thumb along my jaw. "The things I want to do to you," he growled and kissed me again, sucking my bottom lip. "But we have reservations tonight." Trent got up and pulled out wet wipes from his desk drawer. "My predecessor kept these here," he mused. "I didn't think I'd use them."

I started to move, and Trent said, "Stay right there. I'll take care of you." His promise warmed my belly.

"Why do you have to be so perfect?" I mumbled under my breath quietly, not thinking he could hear me.

"I wouldn't go that far, but I do appreciate the compliment."

Trent carefully wiped away any remains of my orgasm. I'd gotten some on my shirt, and he gave me a replacement—one he kept as a backup, just in case. He was prepared for everything. I removed my sweater (I had a T-shirt underneath) and changed quickly into his button-down, wishing it smelled like his cologne and not the detergent from the dry cleaners.

Trent examined me. "It's a little big, but it looks good on you. The bits of green bring out the color of your eyes."

"Glad I wore my contacts."

"I like you in glasses, too." He gathered up his satchel and jacket. "Ready to go?"

My head still swam with lust and confusion as I collected my bag and coat. "Yes," I said as I walked toward the door. Trent placed a hand at the small of my back, only removing it when he locked his office. His touch reassured me, comforted me. Briefly. Stepping out into the sea of cubicles reminded me we were at my father's firm. I was sure having sex in the workplace was frowned upon. I was also pretty sure Trent and I weren't the first ones to do it.

We took the elevator down into the parking garage without saying very much. The ding signaled my floor.

"I'll meet you over there."

"You don't want to ride together?" He seemed disappointed.

"I'd rather not come back here. It's farther from my apartment than the restaurant." It was the truth. The little bit of time it'd take to get from here to the restaurant would clear my head some, too. I needed the distance to think about what we were doing, knowing whatever it was, I didn't want to stop.

THE OLD BIMMER started with a wheeze before turning over, a slight embarrassment compared to Trent's car that purred when he started it. I glanced in my rearview mirror and saw him behind the wheel looking far sexier than any man should. He was powerful and ultrasuccessful. I wasn't sure what he saw in me. Nothing in my life was on track, not like his. He'd finished school. He'd gotten the best job an entertainment attorney could aspire to have. He had the cool car, the nice house—or at least I imagined he did. The only thing I'd done was let those I loved down. My father. My ex. I'd let Melissa down if I didn't figure out a way to pay for tuition. And I'd let Trent down eventually. My life had been on a constant detour because I'd fallen in love, and I had no intention of repeating that mistake. Besides, Trent, no matter how wonderful or perfect, couldn't be serious about being with me. There was too much at risk for him.

"Drop the pity party already," I mumbled as I pulled out onto the main road. The other shoe would drop at some point. It always did. Best thing to do was enjoy the moments I did have with Trent and worry about tomorrow's heartbreak tomorrow.

Panevino was located on the top floor of a skyscraper. Warm tones of red and gold decorated the space combined with portraits of idyllic country scenes and vineyards on the walls. Vegas lights twinkled in the distance, spanning out to where desert landscape met the horizon. The atmosphere was romantic and cozy.

I found Trent in the lounge area, a beautiful room overlooking the cityscape with a bar that had a double-sided gas fireplace, leather couches, and stone tables. Trent smiled when he saw me, kicking up my pulse.

"This view is amazing," he said. "Do you want a drink?"

"A glass of merlot, please."

He went to the bar and ordered for us, and I let the fact I was on an actual date with Trent sink in. With Devon and Carrie, I'd been the one making reservations, holding doors, getting us drinks—things Trent had done without thought. I wondered if he'd order for me, too. I'd never been submissive in my relationships, but I could become extremely attached to being treated this way.

"Here you go." Trent returned with two glasses and handed me one of them. "It's my favorite merlot, so I hope you like it. Cheers." He sat beside me, and we clinked glasses.

I thanked him and took a sip of what was definitely the best merlot I'd ever had. I'd learned about wines from my mother, the connoisseur. My palate was nowhere near her level, but I tasted a blend of spices and subtle woody undertones in Trent's selection. "This is delicious. My mom has a thing for merlot." I took another sip, savoring the taste before swallowing. The thought of my parents' separation darkened my mood. They were divorcing, and it was entirely my father's fault. I'd lost respect for him after mom told me he'd been cheating on her with some woman in Los Angeles that was about my age. How unoriginal. How midlife crisis. And what a crappy thing to do to Mom.

"I met your mother once at a gathering in LA," Trent said, settling into his seat. "She has a lot of spirit and seemed very kind."

"She is. She loves helping people and animals."

"Is she the reason you wanted to become a veterinarian?"

"Probably, but I've always been drawn to animals. Sometimes I think they're better than us humans, you know? Always loving, kind, they don't judge, and always there when you need them."

Trent unexpectedly gave my hand a light squeeze. Bringing my hand to his lips, he kissed the back of it. The affectionate display melted me. Right there. But it was such a bad idea to do PDAs, something Trent must have realized because he let go of my hand and looked around the room.

"I don't see anyone I know, in case that's what you were wondering."

He rubbed his lip. "Yeah, I forgot myself for a minute." An awkward pause came between us. I decided the best thing to do was resume our conversation and try to keep my hands to myself.

"Do you like animals?" I asked.

The question brought a smile to his face. "We had a couple of huskies growing up, and those dogs...they were the best. When I went away to college, I thought about getting a little dog, but decided it'd be unfair. I spent too many hours studying or at the office." He let out a humorless laugh. "My ex, Nic, left me for that same reason. Too many hours neglecting him." Trent took a long pull from his glass, almost draining it.

My mother had suffered similarly. She hated the never-ending hours Dad put into his company, and to compensate, she dove into her real estate business, charities, and women's groups to avoid the loneliness. She was even the president of the local PFLAG chapter for a few years. She never mentioned it to me, but I could always see the sadness in her eyes even when she smiled. I sympathized with Nic. Losing Trent's affection must have cut deeply because he seemed like a brilliant lover, and if this date was an indication of how he treated his boyfriends, he was a romantic at heart.

"How long were you together?"

"A little over seven years. We met just before my freshman year of law school."

"That's a long time." I'd barely lasted two years with Carrie.

Trent finished his wine and gestured to the waitress for another glass.

"Nic is a sore subject. There was more to our breakup than my devotion to my career. He wanted things I couldn't give him."

"Like marriage and kids and stuff?" Someday, I wanted those things.

"No..." Trent paused, as if he was hesitant to continue. "He wanted to be a full-time submissive. I enjoyed the kink on occasion, but I never wanted it to be the backbone of our relationship. So, we reached an impasse." He shrugged. The gesture was more somber than lighthearted, making me think the impasse hurt more than he let on.

"I can't imagine being a Dominant or a sub full-time, but it obviously works for some people, and I think that's pretty cool. It's gotta be liberating trusting someone so completely, having that deep of a commitment to each other and getting to explore each other sexually. You know, I actually read that people in BDSM relationships have the best relationships? They communicate more." I was babbling again. The idea of Trent in leather and ordering me to do...well, anything...excited and enticed me, and pushed every other thought out of my brain. I thought I'd spoken too much, especially the last bit. Obviously Trent's relationship hadn't been the best if they'd broken up.

Tension left Trent's face and shoulders. "I enjoyed what we did at the time, and yeah, there is a deep level of trust and communication involved."

"I think it'd be fun, but I don't think I could do it with just anyone. It'd have to be with someone I trusted, maybe even loved."

"I agree. Georgia, the woman you met in LA, is the only other person I've played with, and that was during training. But some Doms and subs like the voyeuristic aspect of being together. I went to a couple play parties with Nic when we first got into the scene, but then we moved to LA, and I liked keeping what we did between us. It made it more meaningful." Sadness reached his eyes, making it obvious he missed that intimacy with his former lover.

"When I met you, you said you were gay. How does Georgia... I mean, why would you do that, um, training with Georgia?"

"I am gay, but I had no idea how to dominate anyone, and Georgia, who is a full-time Domme, explained the best way to learn was to be a sub first. I trusted her, and to me, that was more important than anything else. Nic would tell me what he was interested in trying, and Georgia would demonstrate it on me, and then teach me how to do it to him."

"That is...so hot."

He had a beautiful, heartfelt laugh. "It is and was. But more than that, I liked making Nic happy and wanted to learn how to please him properly, to explore his fantasies and mine without serious injury."

"Serious injury?" I parroted like an idiot.

"Yeah, well, sometimes things don't go as planned. The more preparation and knowledge I had about the scene we were going to do, the more comfortable I felt about dominating. Not everyone feels that way. Georgia likes to improvise and stretch her sub's limits, which makes her good at being a Domme. I had a harder time with it."

"What...um...what did you like to do?" The image of him wielding chains and leather, rendering me powerless while doing so, gripped me, making my skinny jeans skinnier in the worst place.

"For the most part, what I like is considered vanilla kink. Spanking, bondage, occasional breath play. And I love using toys. But I think I have a new thing for men dressed in women's clothes." He winked. There was an excitement in his tone I hadn't heard before. "But underlying all of it was my love for Nic, making sure I balanced any pain with pleasure."

"That sounds incredibly sweet."

"It was, at first. Nic's tastes changed over the years. He preferred extensive verbal humiliation—being degraded, called names. But for me…" He looked away, swirling the last drops of wine in his glass. "It crossed a line, a hard limit, something I couldn't do. Don't get me wrong, I do like some humiliation—you licking your come off my hand, for instance, is a form of it."

My body temperature spiked, and I stuck a finger under my collar, loosening it. "I liked that, too."

"I'm glad you feel that way. I suspected you had a predilection for a little pain with your pleasure, given your tattoos and strategic piercings."

*Great.* My semi went full, and a waitress was walking toward us. I couldn't adjust it without being obvious.

"This might be weird to say, but I'm sorry it didn't work out for you guys. You seem like you really loved him."

"Thank you. I did, but when we moved to LA, I worked longer hours, trying to make junior partner before I turned thirty. In turn, he demanded more play time, and honestly, I was too tired to deal." Trent scratched his eyebrow, deep in thought. "Eventually, I didn't want to come home at all, knowing he'd be there waiting for it. Sex felt more like a chore, and that was unfair to both of us."

"When Carrie and I got engaged, my mom said, 'Relationships are what we put into them, and if only one person is putting something in, they don't work.' Carrie wanted to stay in Vegas, so I went to school here and pursued law. Carrie wanted a nicer apartment, so we found one. Carrie wanted a big wedding, so we planned one. Carrie wanted a better car, so we bought one. I never stopped to think about what I wanted and neither did she, until it involved my sexuality." I had a point in there somewhere.

"Is that why you were defensive when you said you were bisexual?"

"Yeah, sorry. Guess that's a touchy thing for me. She thought I'd eventually want to be with a man—that she wouldn't be enough—so she called off the engagement. Looking back, there was so much more wrong with our relationship."

The hostess approached and said our table was ready. Trent waited for me to stand and let me go first, placing his hand on the small of my back like he'd done the first night we were together. I loved the way he treated me like I was something precious.

Our table was next to the window and we had a panoramic view of the Strip. The illuminated skyline was romantic from this distance, far detached from the party vibe and crowds that went with being on Las Vegas Boulevard.

We reviewed the menu and ordered, making small talk about the restaurant and its décor afterward. Being around Trent was easier than I'd anticipated. I loved his candor and his gentleness. Most of the attorneys I'd met had an arrogance to them—a kill or be killed attitude. Trent wore confidence, not arrogance, and it was done in a calm and open manner, which made him such a hottie.

He rested his arms on the table and folded his hands. "Can I ask you something? Why are you not doing well in law school? You're obviously smart. Melissa told me you graduated at the top of your class last year and excelled on your LSAT."

"Is this the mentoring part of our date?"

"Humor me."

"I just can't seem to find any motivation. I mean, what good is being a lawyer when the justice system sucks so hard? No offense, but the legal system has nothing to do with justice; it's about who can find loopholes in the law to get the outcome they want." After seeing what Devon had gone through, the criminal justice system needed a severe overhaul. And corporate law was no better. Those lawyers just made more money and backhanded deals that ended up hurting people by demanding arbitration, and that resolution was so whack, the average person hardly ever won.

"Jaded views aside," he said with an amused grin, "I suspect there's another reason."

"Please, enlighten me." If he was set on playing mentor, I could easily play the part of snarky mentee. I took a long drink. Two glasses of wine without food and I was starting to get a little buzzed.

"My sister said she helped you get into UC Davis and that you were accepted. She also said you'd make an amazing veterinarian."

"Your sister is kind."

"Ha!" He barked a laugh, showing off his smile and those sexy white teeth. *Such a weird turn-on.* "My sister is a hard ass. She doesn't dole out support or compliments if she doesn't believe in someone."

Our dinner salads and a basket of garlic bread arrived, interrupting briefly. Trent thanked the waiter and then snagged a piece of the bread.

"Your sister has a big mouth," I mumbled. "Yeah, I got accepted."

"When do you start?"

"I could take summer classes or start in September." I poked at my food with my fork. "But I can't go, not yet. I have to find a job and get some money saved before I can."

"You don't think your parents will help you pay for tuition?"

"Dad wants me to take on the family business. So, no, I don't think he'll help. Mom might be able to lend me some of it."

"What if we found another way for you to afford to go? Scholarships, grants, loans, work-study. There are other means."

I hated the little bit of hope that sprang up. "We? You'd help me?"

"Isn't that my job as your mentor? I'll do some research this week and talk with Melissa to see if she has any suggestions. You should contact UC Davis and find out the process for applying for scholarships, loans, and work-study."

"Way to ruin the feels I was getting." I stabbed at a tomato on his plate and popped it in my mouth.

"I don't know whether to kiss you or spank you."

"Fascinating mentoring technique. Let's try both. See which one works better."

"Deal." He held me with an affectionate gaze.

"I'd so kiss you right now if you hadn't eaten all that garlic bread."

He laughed. "Does that mean you'll accept my help?"

"Yes!" With Trent's support, my goal no longer seemed like a pipe dream. He'd give me the kick in the butt I needed to at least see what my options were. But hope was a scary thing. It once had me convinced I'd be married and become a veterinarian, and that'd all been ripped away. Still, Trent's confidence and desire for me—not some version of me like my ex had dreamed up—had me believing I could do this. I finally had someone who liked me for me and seemed to want to help me make my dream come true.

I also had someone who could break me into tiny unfixable pieces if he walked away.

# Chapter Fourteen

Trenton

Oisin and I were leaving the restaurant just as two middle-aged women dressed in elegant evening dresses were entering. One of them stopped us.

"Oisin Harrison? It's been ages."

For a fraction of a heartbeat, he straightened like a kid caught doing something he shouldn't, and then donned a slightly forced expression of ease.

"Mrs. Bryant, good to see you."

Mrs. Bryant—as in the senior partner's wife, Bryant. I hadn't met the woman, only her husband. No wonder Oisin had gone rigid. The unexpected encounter underscored how small a town Vegas was, and how far a reach Harrison, Preston, and Bryant, Inc. had.

"And who is this lovely gentleman with you?" She cocked an eyebrow and proffered her hand.

"Trenton Fisher."

"Oh, yes, Mr. Fisher. My husband mentioned you'd relocated to our little neck of the woods. How fortunate to have met you here." She darted her eyes back and forth between Oisin and me. "I trust Oisin is giving you a tour of our fair city?" Curiosity rang in her voice. I was about to answer her when Oisin surprised me by speaking up.

"My father asked Mr. Fisher if he'd mind helping me with my contracts class. As I'm sure you've heard, Mr. Fisher is phenomenal when it comes to contracts and negotiations." He delivered the truth with a smile and boosted my ego in the process. He must have picked up on her judgmental undertone as well.

"I see. What a terribly romantic spot to be discussing contracts." That scrutinizing eyebrow lifted again.

"Best vegetarian lasagna in town. I couldn't resist," Oisin replied with a shrug. "Well, we have to get going. It was nice seeing you again, Mrs. Bryant. I'll be sure to tell my mother you said hello."

"It was nice meeting you, Mrs. Bryant."

"You too, Mr. Fisher." The woman was frostier than a frozen beer mug.

When we got outside, Oisin clasped his elbows, drawing in on himself.

"I can't do anything in this city without running into someone my father knows. If this gets back to him, he might give you some hideous punishment or transfer you to Guam."

"I'm not licensed to practice in Guam, so I think I'm safe there. Alaska? That might be more of a concern." I started walking toward my car.

"You know what I mean."

It was all I could do not to kiss him; he looked so damn cute. "I do, and you're right. But I'm one of those lawyers you seem to detest, and I'm quite good at finding loopholes. Should your father say anything to me about tonight, I'll tell him a version of the truth that's convincing."

"Like what?"

"Like, you're a vegetarian, something I'm sure he knows, and you recommended this place. He never said I couldn't eat with you."

"If those are your mad persuasive skills, I don't know how you got promoted so quickly."

"You haven't seen me in action."

He laughed. "Oh, I've seen you in action. So has the couch in your office."

"The couch didn't mind, and neither did you." Our office sexcapade wasn't the wisest of actions, though well worth it. I'd been too eager to watch him fly apart as Oisin, not Sin. After our discussion at dinner, I had no reason to think I'd made the wrong choice by advancing on him. Oisin had been receptive, curious, and exuberant about everything, including when I offered to help him with UC Davis. I already knew if other funds weren't available, I'd lend him the money. Or gift it. I'd decide later.

"Um, no. I didn't mind." His hazel eyes sparkled.

"I didn't think so." I got my car keys out. "You're not driving home, by the way."

"I'm not?"

"No. I'm taking you."

"What about my car?"

"I'll pick you up before work tomorrow so you can get it. You're a little too intoxicated, and I don't feel comfortable with you driving." Perhaps I'd overstepped. I'd grown possessive, concerned, and attached to this young man in a matter of days. Oisin only had a few drinks over the course of the meal and was probably safe to drive. Mostly, I was unwilling to end our time together.

"I don't think I've ever had anyone care for me like you do, Trent, and you barely know me." He reached for my hand and stopped himself. That changed when we got in my car and drove to his apartment holding hands the entire time.

"This is me," he said as we pulled up to a sterile-looking apartment complex. I suppose the son of a multimillionaire could live anywhere he desired. Perhaps this military-styled housing was his choice, but he deserved more. A nice home with a yard for a dog. I resisted the impulse to turn the car around and drive Oisin to my house. Then what? Ask him to move in? Too much. Too soon.

"Are you free on Saturday?" I had to let him go, but come the weekend, I'd like a chance to wake up next to him.

"I have a study group at eight—they're masochists and not in the fun way." He blushed. "But my afternoon's open. Why? Do I need another 'mentoring session' with you?"

"Actually, I had something else in mind. I'd like to take you out again, and I have an idea on how we can do it without worrying about people from the office recognizing you. Does anyone besides Devon know what you look like as Sin?"

A light shone in his eyes. He liked the idea.

"No. Devon has this whole new makeup thing and none of my family has seen it on me yet. It's perfect!" He grabbed my face and kissed me, and I was swept away in the taste of him as our tongues met. Wet. Sloppy. Desperate. Made my dick hard in an instant.

"I'll see what Devon's up to this weekend. Maybe he can even teach me how to do it, so I wouldn't have to bother him every time we wanted to go out." He beamed, and I liked that he envisioned a future for us.

I caressed his bottom lip with my thumb and forced his mouth open. Without instruction, he wrapped his lips around it and started to suck. The combined sight of his heavy-lidded eyes and the memory of the blow job at the hotel had my cock punching at the fly of my pants.

He released my thumb and eyed my crotch. "I could take care of that, if you wanted."

*I wanted. Oh, man, did I want.* "I think being in a parked car outside your apartment isn't the wisest place for this to be addressed."

He stuck out that pouty, pierced lip and made puppy-dog eyes for the second time. "Neither was your office."

Dammit, he was too cute. "It's probably best not to do anything in public that would get us arrested."

He slouched in his seat. "You're right.

"Besides, it'll give us something to look forward to this weekend."

"I'll definitely be looking forward to it this weekend and anything else you might have planned, Teach," he added with a mischievous grin.

"You don't even know what you're asking for."

"I'm asking for you to have your way with me. A little pain, a little pleasure." Oisin kissed me again, no tongue. "But you're right. I really don't know what I'm asking for." He turned his head and looked at his apartment building. "I should go. Thanks for dinner, and I'll text you in the morning about getting my car." After a final swift kiss on the lips, he exited the car.

I stayed until he got safely into the building before driving away.

# Chapter Fifteen

OISIN

It was the end of the week, and I'd officially been put on academic probation and advised to withdraw from my property law and civil procedure classes to avoid failing grades. That left my contracts class, which I actually liked. A few pretentious classmates had heard the news. They gloated to my face that the son of such a prominent attorney was a fucked up tattooed, pierced homo. Explaining I was bi was a waste of breath on those troglodytes. Regardless, my father would hear of it, and I expected a phone call or visit over the weekend and another lecture about my failures and flaws. What really sucked was all of this had the potential of screwing up my weekend plans with Trent.

Devon opened my door just as I put the key in to unlock it. He was in full makeup and wearing a gorgeous blue dress—far more put together than when I'd seen him on Wednesday. I'd texted him earlier and asked him to come over and bring his makeup kit, explaining that I'd like to learn how to do it myself. He was so excited, he didn't ask why. Usually he was all up in my business, but I never minded. Nothing felt real unless I told him, and I had a lot to share.

"I hope you don't mind me letting myself in. I brought Chinese food and got you the veggie stir-fry with tofu." The breakfast bar was set, and our dinner remained in take-out containers. "I also brought my makeup kit, like you asked, and a change of clothes for you. It's another Goth-like outfit with buckles and zippers to die for. Not as flashy as the last one, but I thought you'd look fantastic in it."

Devon frequently bought my clothing—for which I always reimbursed him—as I'd learned long ago that I trusted his fashion sense over my own. He had a far better eye than I did for putting together outfits that looked good on me, and it was something he liked doing.

I hugged him. "That's super sweet of you, Dev. Thanks." I took off my coat and put my satchel on my desk.

Devon opened the containers and filled our plates without saying a word. The more I examined my friend, the more I suspected something wasn't right. I hoped I hadn't given him bad advice and that maybe he and Stone hadn't been able to work things out after all.

"What's going on?"

He circled a few noodles around his fork, staring down at his food. "A couple things, actually." He worried his bottom lip. "I've been doing some thinking about how I identify."

"Yeah? Sexy Dungeon Master isn't working for you anymore?"

He smiled. "I'll never give up that title, but as for my mundane identity—"

"You're anything but mundane."

"Oh, you're so good for my ego." He gestured for me to lean in and gave me a kiss on the lips. "Seriously, though, I've decided to identify as genderfluid."

"Are you changing your pronouns, too?" Most of the time Devon went with he/him, but when we'd go out dancing he'd occasionally use she/her.

"I don't know yet, probably just whatever suits my mood for now. I'm still figuring this out, you know? You're the second person I've told. Stone was the first, and he said it didn't matter to him how I identified as long as it made me happy."

I think I liked Stone even more.

"That's good, right?"

"It is." He picked at his food.

"What else is going on?"

"I told Charlie I'd do it—take over the shop. He said he'd still be there from time to time, but he's hoping by next year he can retire and transfer the ownership to me."

Ever since I'd known Devon, which was about seven years, his passion had been cars, and not just any cars. He loved classic and vintage ones. I hadn't known there was a difference until he told me. His dream had come true, and he should've been jumping up and down with excitement, not moping in his lo mein.

"That's great news. We should celebrate!"

"It is," he said with a sigh. "I haven't told Stone about the shop, not yet. It's just going to create more of a divide between us."

"Because he wants you to move to LA?"

"I don't want to live there, Os. Like you said before, Vegas is my home. I love my job, and now I've been handed my dream gig. I just can't drop everything and live off Stone while I try to find some entry-level bullshit position in LA." He raked his fingers through his hair, messing up the gelled style. "I'm still not convinced living together is a good move."

"Have you guys talked about any of this?"

"Not yet. He'll be here this weekend, and I'll have to talk about it then."

"What if he could get the band to come up here and record a few songs? That way you guys could do a test run of living together. I hear the Palms hotel has an amazing recording studio."

"I'll mention it to him." He rested his chin in his hand and continued to stir his food without eating it. "It doesn't solve the other things, like the paparazzi and rabid fans." Devon's sunshine disposition hit a negative storm front, which was completely unlike my bestie.

I got up and wrapped my arms around him. "Of all the people I know, Dev, you have the most confidence and the best 'fuck 'em all' attitude. Don't let the paps or the fans ruin your chance at happiness. They don't deserve that. Stone, on the other hand, deserves your love. He could've kept your relationship hidden. He could've done the whole scared of what the public thought about him being with you thing. But what did he do the second he decided he liked you?"

"He got an apartment in Vegas so we could date."

"And he's affectionate in public. And he's introduced you to his family. He's crazy about you. He's shown some real effort. I have no doubt he's going to bend over backward to make things work between you two. If he can get the band to come here, you should give living together a shot. What have you got to lose by trying?"

"I've got more to lose by not trying, don't I? I love him. Being together is harder than I thought, that's all." He took a deep breath. "After the thing with Jerry went down, Stone wanted to hire a security guard to shadow me. I didn't let him. It felt kinda foolish, you know?"

"That was months ago, before word got out about the two of you dating. Do you think you'd feel better if you let him hire someone to protect you now?"

"I guess so. I have so much to talk to him about. It's hard being separated most of the time because when I see him, I don't want to talk. I want to do other things that are more fun and involve naked time."

"Completely understandable." I squeezed him and returned to my seat. "Why don't you take him someplace semipublic and quiet like a park so you can talk without the temptation of naked time?"

"That's a good idea, even if it's not as much fun."

"For what it's worth, I think he's going to support your decision to take over the shop. After all, it means free repairs for Matty's Pontiac." The keyboard player of Stone's Army loved that car. But for Stone and Devon, it'd been the start of their relationship. If Jerry hadn't smashed it up, Matty and Stone wouldn't have brought it to the specialty shop where Devon worked, and Stone wouldn't have gotten a chance to ask him out.

Devon snorted. "I'm sure that's exactly why Stone would support me."

"It's going to be okay, Dev." I shoved some food into my mouth, not sure what else to say.

"I hope so." He finally took a bite of his lo mein. "Why did you want me to bring my makeup kit over? Have I converted you completely?" He grinned.

"Trent asked me out, like on a real date, and I thought if I could learn how to apply the makeup, I'd avoid Dad's spies."

"You guys have been going out together all week. Why care now?"

"Monday, I had no idea I was meeting him, and Wednesday was our scheduled mentoring session."

Devon snickered. "He mentored you in the fine art of hand jobs."

"Don't make me regret telling you." I scowled.

"Puh-leeze," Devon said, pointing his fork at me. "You couldn't keep something that delicious to yourself."

"True."

"A little mystery, a little undercover romance, and a taboo love affair. You have all the fun." A big dimpled smile finally appeared.

"I suppose." When Trent mentioned me dressing as Sin as a way for us to go around undetected together, I thought it was a good idea. But without Devon joining me, it seemed strange.

"We always do dress up together, you know? I'm gonna miss you."

Devon came up behind me and gave me a hug. "It's time to take the training bra off." He chuckled as I swatted him.

"Fine, mock me," I said dramatically, making Devon break out into a full laugh.

"You got the queen part down. Guess we gotta work on the drag part now."

"The date is in the afternoon, and I was hoping for less drag queen, more normal. Maybe like the kilt thing we did on Saturday?"

He scrunched his face. "Basically, you want the guyliner look with flair?"

"I guess."

He put a finger to his chin, gazing at the ceiling in contemplation.

"Don't hurt yourself. You might get a brain cramp thinking that hard."

He narrowed his eyes, looking like a cat ready to strike. "Bitch," he teased. "Do you want my help or not?"

I chuckled. "Yes, I do."

"Then let the master do her thing." Devon was in serious diva mode.

"How about something I can wear Converse with, or anything besides those high-heeled boots."

"You're pathetic. There was barely a heel on them."

"Five inches isn't shabby." I busted out laughing as my prepubescent brain took over. "Five inches is kinda pathetic."

"Glad you said it." He raked his hands through his already messy hair. The remaining product in it made it stand straight up. "Okay, I've got it! Let's go raid your closet, and anything you don't have, I'll bring over later. Do you still have the makeup I bought you in LA?"

"Yeah."

He clapped his hands together. "Let's do this!"

# Chapter Sixteen

OISIN

Saturday. I stared at my reflection in the bathroom mirror and shook my head. "This is useless." I'd spent hours trying to apply the makeup the way Devon had shown me and all I'd done was make myself look like a creature from a horror film. Guyliner and lipstick I could do. This contouring stuff was for the experts. Devon could've fixed this mess on my face in less than a half hour. If he and Stone weren't going through such a rough patch, I'd have begged him to come over.

Devon. This entire routine felt entirely too empty without him. And wrong. All this effort was supposed to lead to dancing and fun with my best friend. This was our thing. Girls Night Out had more meaning than just us looking fancy; it was a symbol of our friendship, and using it as a mask to change who I was, stung. That was starting to be too strong a theme in my life.

"I give up." For the fifth time, I scrubbed the makeup off my face using the wipes Devon had left behind. Not only was the makeup difficult to apply, it stuck to my face like superglue. The wipes got the majority of it off, the rest washed away after using a combination of lotion and soap. None of the makeup I used normally was this stubborn to remove.

Ditching the original plan altogether, I donned a pair of skinny jeans and a T-shirt with a sweater over it. The boy shorts stayed. They were form fitting with light blue lace on the sides and a cute ribbon tying up the front. I liked them. They made me feel sexy, all the good parts of dressing femme without the makeup woes. This was me, and I felt comfortable in my own skin for the first time that day.

My eyes itched and were bloodshot from all the makeup. The final transformation from Sin to Oisin took place as I removed the colored contacts and put on my glasses. Voila. Oisin Harrison, Emo Nerd at

Large once again. I had to tell Trent I'd failed and couldn't meet him. Frustrated and annoyed, I typed the text to Trent and sent it.

*I still look like me. I had a makeup fail, and Devon isn't available. We should cancel and just meet for "mentoring" on Wednesday.*

I waited for his response, feeling my throat constrict as I tried to hold back my disappointment. I refused to get upset. I'd see him Wednesday. It wasn't a big deal... I was no good at talking myself out of feeling crappy. I'd been looking forward to this date for what felt like an eternity.

When my phone chirped, my pulse went into full throttle.

*Let's meet today anyway. We can go to the Hoover Dam or someplace out of town where we won't be recognized.*

"Yes!" I fist pumped the air and quickly texted him back, giving him the location of a nearby pub, adding I'd meet him out front. I'd been there once and it definitely catered to the jocks, not the law students. I figured I wouldn't be recognized during daylight hours, unlike my apartment where several future lawyers resided.

My phone chirped again.

*Bring an overnight bag. I'll pick you up at 1:30.*

Oh hell yeah! I texted him a smiley face.

I gathered up a change of clothes, including a pair of track pants to sleep in, not that I expected to use them, and had time to make a peanut butter and jelly sandwich to tide me over for the next hour while I waited for Trent.


WHEN I ARRIVED at the pub, I saw Trent leaning against the wall, checking his phone and looking sexy as heck in dark denim and a black peacoat. I resisted the urge to run up to him, hug him, and kiss him. That was the kind of person I'd been with Carrie. I'd constantly embarrassed her with my affection. She pretended to be bothered by it, but she wasn't. I tempered the blossoming happiness, congratulating myself at how well I'd done controlling my urges.

Trent smiled when he saw me, and I returned it, feeling the warmth of his gaze. "You look nice." He reached for me and ended up raising his hand higher to pat me on the arm. The gesture was entirely awkward, and I had to laugh.

"You too," I replied and imitated him, adding more of a hesitation for show.

He chuckled. "I thought you looked hot dressed as Sin, but those glasses are adorable. Makes it hard for me to resist touching you the way I want to."

"Maybe we should leave so you can?"

"I couldn't agree more. I'm parked right there." He motioned to his car, which was parked a few feet away. We cleared the distance quickly, and he opened the passenger side door.

"Such a gentleman."

"Always."

The sunny weather was bound to make the hour-long drive to the Hoover Dam a pleasant one. Trent had booked a room at the nearby Boulder Dam Hotel for the night, and I couldn't wait to have him inside me again. *Skip the dam; let's get to the good stuff.* Especially after all that talk about the less than vanilla things he used to do.

Fifteen minutes into the drive, I got a phone call. My palms started sweating as soon as I heard the "Imperial March" ringtone.

"It's my father. If I don't get it, he'll be upset." I hadn't told Trent I'd had to drop two of my three classes if I wanted to maintain an acceptable GPA, or that I'd have to retake the courses over the summer. The thought made me sick.

Trent licked his lips. "He has no way of knowing you're with me or what we're up to. Don't sweat it." The white around Trent's knuckles as he gripped the steering wheel indicated he wasn't half as calm about my father's interruption as he'd like me to believe.

After taking a deep breath, I answered my phone.

"Do you know who I spoke with a few minutes ago?" Dad's patronizing tone grated on me. "Your academic advisor. And do you know what he said?"

*Probably something like: Why are you bothering me on a Saturday?*

I remained silent. I didn't feel the need to contribute to this conversation; Dad was doing fine on his own.

"He said that you've withdrawn from your classes and are performing at the bottom twenty percentile of your class."

That was higher than I'd thought.

"I know," I muttered.

"You know? With all the help I've gotten you, you decided to give up? Oisin, what is going on with you? Your mother and I are half out of our minds with worrying, not knowing if you're on drugs or if you've fallen into a bad situation. You were a straight A student all through college, and now you're throwing your life away, and I can't figure out why or what happened."

"I don't want to talk about it." I stared out the window at the desert landscape racing by, hoping cell service would cut out.

"If it's not drugs or drinking, then is it some sort of sexual identity crisis?"

"What? Why would you think that?"

"If you need help, Oisin, we can get you into counseling. I read transgender members of the community have the highest suicide rate, and if that's what you are then—"

"I'm not transgender, I'm bisexual. I've told you that." Not that he ever understood it.

"Then what is going on? Talk to me, Os."

I huffed as the truth boiled under my skin. "You cheated on Mom. You left this family when you went off with that woman. That's what's going on. You constantly treat me like an infant, calling my professors, making me go to counseling and tutoring. Jesus, Dad, you even made your own employee, a soon-to-be partner, babysit me. I'm freaking twenty-two years old, not five. I can make my own decisions, and if I want to fuck up my life, then that's my choice." Every part of my body vibrated with anger and adrenaline. I'd never spoken to my father like that before.

"If that's how you really feel"—he seethed—"then you can screw your life up without my financial support or your trust."

"Fine! I don't want your money anyway! It's done nothing but make this family miserable."

"Consider yourself liberated. I'll have the papers drawn up and sent to you first thing Monday morning."

"Whatever. Bye." I hung up and threw my phone into the backseat.

I was trembling inside and out. I shoved my hands over my face and doubled over in the seat, trying to wrap my head around what had happened. I'd been cut off. I had no money. I had no school. I had no security.

"Oisin?" Trent asked, lightly placing his hand on my back.

I started laughing—hard and hysterically—and then sat up. "What have I done, Trent? Dad just cut me off." I laughed some more. I hadn't laughed this hard in a long time. I remembered Stone had called me the "Emo hyena" when he first met Dev and me. I *was* laughing just like a hyena.

"Take a deep breath," Trent said using his deep, commanding voice. "You're going to be fine. I've got you."

"Oh no!" I spat. "No, no. You do not have me. I'm done with people controlling me with their money, or their mind games, or whatever. I'm done. I'm going to live for me now. Not you. Not my dad. Not my mom. Just me. Turn the car around."

"What?"

"You heard me! Turn the fucking car around!" I grabbed the steering wheel and the car veered off the road into the breakdown lane. Trent slammed on the breaks, sending me flying forward, but the seatbelt caught me before I hit the dashboard.

"You need to calm the fuck down, right now," Trent bellowed.

"I'm sorry." I wrapped my arms around myself, coming back to my senses. "I'm so sorry. I've never spoken like that to my father before... And I didn't meant it—the part about being done with you or you not having me." I forced myself to look at him. "You do have me. You're all I can think about, and I'm sorry if I messed that up." I searched his face, hoping he'd say I was forgiven.

Trent unfastened his seatbelt and mine and held me. Placing a tender kiss on the top of my head, he kept me in his arms for a few breaths, soothing my nerves. "You were right to stand up to him."

"Thank you."

"Can I suggest something, however? The next time you decide to stand up for yourself, you do it without the near-fatal car crash?"

I let out a nervous laugh. "I'm sorry I freaked out."

"You're forgiven," he said and took possession of my mouth, knocking my glasses to the side. *Damn he can kiss.* My toes curled inside my Converse.

"Buckle up." He sat back and fastened his seatbelt.

"Where are we going?"

"We're going to go see the Hoover Dam, like we planned."

I ran my hand up his thigh and across his crotch. Palming him, I rubbed his girth until he groaned. The urge to taste him grabbed hold of me. I had to do it. Maybe it was left over adrenaline rush or a need to bring utter chaos into my life. A blow job at seventy-five miles an hour was a completely stupid idea—and I was hell-bent on doing it.

I unfastened the button to his pants and unzipped him. "You'd better drive safe. Keep it well within the speed limit because I'm gonna suck you off." I removed my glasses and had his entire dick down before he could protest.

He hissed. "Damn, boy. Fuck!"

I reached between his legs and played with his balls, lightly squeezing and rolling them as much as I could in the confined space. The engine roared as I brushed against his hole. I popped off his dick. "Careful, now. Wouldn't want to crash the car."

Laughing, he shoved my head back down on his cock. "Don't you dare stop."

His husky voice shot right to my groin, and I pinched it, shifting it to the side to give it some room to grow. Hollowing out my cheeks, I sucked Trent's monster boner, loving how his thick shaft forced my lips to stretch to take all of him. With one finger curled inside his hole, I took Trent into my throat and gagged when I went too deep. I kept going, though, determined to milk him by contracting my throat muscles around him. *Who needs to breathe?*

"Fuck, yeah!" He thrust up to meet me, and the car jumped forward. *Someone had hit the gas pedal.*

I hummed, bringing him as far down into my throat as I could. Yeah, giving head ruled. Wrapping my fingers around the base of his shaft, I pumped him, savoring the strong flavor of his pre-come as it burst into my mouth. He was close.

"That's it, baby. Don't stop. Don't you dare fucking stop."

*Not on your life.*

I stroked faster, rubbing the vein along his shaft with my thumb as I pressed my lips tight around his width. Up down up down. His thigh muscles tightened; his abs clenched.

"*Fuuuuuuukk!*"

Hot come splashed down my throat, and I greedily swallowed all of it, savoring his cock until it went semi-soft.

The car slowed down, and I sat up. Wiping my mouth, I looked at my lover. His eyes remained hazy in postorgasmic bliss. I remained rock hard and unbuttoned my pants, ready to take care of that problem.

"What are you doing?" he asked.

"Kinda obvious, don't ya think?" I pushed my fly down.

"That's mine, Os. Don't you dare touch it until I say you can."

"This part of the kink you like?"

"You'll like it too, I promise. Just wait."

"I'm not patient."

"Try to control yourself."

"Is this punishment?"

"No. You'll know if I intend to punish you. This is to give you more pleasure, trust me."

I gave myself one final adjustment and zipped back up. "I trust you."

# Chapter Seventeen

TRENTON

We stood on top of the dam admiring Lake Mead. The brisk wind left no doubt it was wintertime and had turned Oisin's cheeks and the tips of his ears a rosy pink.

"Have you been here before?" I asked.

"Yeah, a couple times. Family vacation when I was about twelve, and then my mom took Devon and me a year later." He turned to face me. "You?"

"High school field trip. Back then water levels were higher."

"During the Paleolithic era?"

"Your history is terrible. This lake wasn't even here—"

"Mesolithic?"

"You're hilarious."

"And cold. Think we've had enough sightseeing? I mean, the Colorado River is fascinating and all, but I'd really love to be naked in a nice warm bath with a sexy older man."

"Are you sure you want to be with a man from the Stone Age?"

"As long as he has ginger facial hair and sexy teeth, I'm in."

"Sexy teeth? You think my *teeth* are sexy?"

"Among other things, yes. Oh, and he has to have a monster co— Oh shit."

I followed the direction of Oisin's stare and saw a young woman and man taking a selfie. They were laughing and exchanged a kiss before she turned our way. She held up her finger, signaling her lover to wait, and then headed toward us.

"What a crazy coincidence," she said to Oisin before shifting her green eyes on me. Being jealous over a woman was a new experience for me. I'd believed I was immune to such insecurities, that I was better than all the other guys who complained that they'd never date someone who was bisexual because they'd always be wondering if they were enough. But the hundred and ten pounds or so of woman standing in front of me seemed formidable. I was relieved when she redirected her attention on Oisin.

"Isn't it, though." His response was flat.

"I've been thinking about you lately. When you didn't show up at my father's funeral…"

"My family sent flowers." Oisin fidgeted.

"And they were beautiful. I just thought you'd come."

"I'm sorry your father passed, Carrie."

"He liked you, you know."

"I liked him. He was a good guy."

An awkward silence descended among us, making it clear introductions weren't going to be made.

"I guess I'll see you around?"

"Yeah. Probably."

She nodded and returned to her lover's arms.

Oisin walked away from me without a word. I gave him his space, not catching up with him until he reached the car.

"That was Carrie."

"You don't say."

"I'm sorry I didn't introduce you. I wasn't thinking." He raked his hands through his hair. "Fuck! We can't go *anywhere* without someone recognizing me. With the way today is going, I wouldn't be surprised if she and Ken, or Keith—whatever the fuck his name is—are staying at the same hotel as us."

"Are you over her?" The ridiculous question left my mouth before I could stop it.

"What? Yeah, of course." His tone was too high.

"It's okay if you're not." No, it was not okay, but considering he was engaged only five months ago, I could understand. "You shared your life with her, and she has things that you might miss."

"Like what? Her controlling me? Her dictating my life and making me miserable? No, there's nothing I miss about that relationship."

"Like the fact that she's a woman and…"

Oisin froze. "Seriously?"

"I didn't expect to be jealous—"

"Stop. Just stop." He held up his hands. "If you think I'm only attracted to cis men and women, then you've misunderstood what it means to be bisexual. If you're gonna be all jealous, then you should be jealous of Devon, too—he's genderfluid. But you know what? None of it fucking matters because I'm with *you*."

I'd wounded him, probably in the worst of ways, and I needed to take that pain away.

"I'm sorry." I went to him, and no longer caring that we were in public, wrapped him in my arms. He returned my embrace without hesitating, nuzzling into my neck until his breathing slowed down.

"We barely know each other," he said softly, "and I can see why you'd be upset by meeting my ex. That's pretty normal. I'm just tired of having to defend my sexuality. I even had to do it with Devon recently, so you just hit a sore spot."

I held him tighter, apologizing once more, adding, "It's all your fault really."

"How is it all my fault?" He tried to move out of my arms, but I didn't let go.

"If you weren't so damn sexy and irresistible, I wouldn't be so jealous. I wouldn't want you all to myself."

"And you wouldn't be risking your job to spend time with me."

"No, I wouldn't."

"Can we go to the hotel now? I bet our make up sex is going to be amazing."

I just fell a little deeper for Oisin Harrison.

SUNLIGHT FRAMED THE curtains and spilled into the room, revealing the disarray of clothing on the floor beside the bed along with used towels, lube, and condoms. The smell of sex hung in the air, and the room's heater had kicked on and off all night, thickening the odor. Oisin remained in my arms, one leg over mine, making it impossible to move without waking him. But I had no intention of moving. Having him close to me, naked and sleeping, felt amazing. Sex with Oisin was a gift, and the previous night I'd had him begging and pleading to come, his cock dripping with need.

Oisin's breathing became shallower as he stirred awake. "What time is it?" He snuggled closer. In turn, I hugged him tighter, feeling sweat form along our torsos.

"It's almost nine." I never slept that late anymore. Usually, I'd get up to go to the gym or run before work.

"What time do we have to leave?"

"Checkout is at eleven."

He shifted, propping himself up on an elbow to face me. "That sucks. Only two hours and then back to...whatever."

"Whatever? No. You said you'd finish out the semester and save up for UC Davis, like we talked about at dinner last night."

"What if I don't come up with tuition? What if I can't afford to move? What if—"

I kissed him to quiet his demons of insecurity. "Stop. We'll find a way for you to go, remember?"

"Okay. Thank you." He straddled me, lining up our cocks, and began canting his hips. I loved how he took charge. Nic never would have. Nothing wrong with frotting, and Oisin's piercings rubbing against my sensitive flesh made it better.

"Do you ever bottom?" he asked, wrapping a hand around both our dicks and lazily stroking.

"Not since college." My dick thickened, voicing its opinion before I'd made up my mind. Nic and I had experimented when we first started dating, and I hadn't enjoyed it as much as I'd hoped. Nic liked to bottom, so the issue never resurfaced. "Do you typically bottom?"

He flushed. "Um... You were the first guy I let top me."

"I was? Why me?" I'd been the only one to lay claim to that hot ass, and fuck if that didn't send a primal surge to my ego.

"When we were hanging out at the club, you held on to me. You kept touching me, guiding me through the crowd, out of the club, into the hotel lobby. You had—and have—this quiet confidence about you that convinced me you'd be a good lover. I was right by the way. Not to mention, you're hellasexy. I love this beard." He scratched my jaw. "Plus, I had that dress on and felt pretty feminine."

"A little role-play fantasy then?"

"I suppose. I mean, I'd never had sex dressed up like that before. But it was more how you treated me that night that made me brave enough to try. The lingerie was a fun bonus, that's all."

"Come here," I said and pulled him against me. "I loved you in that outfit. I'd never been with anyone like that before, and it was hotter than hell. Knowing I was your first, I...I wish you'd have told me."

Oisin rested on his forearms, leaning over me. "Would you have treated me any different? You gave me a massage, took a long time with prep—it's like you knew to be gentle or something. I was so relaxed by the time we fucked that there was almost no burn. You felt amazing, Trent, and I wouldn't change a thing about that night."

Mine. That ass was all mine and mine alone. I *was* a possessive caveman; I had to claim him again. I clutched Oisin and flipped him onto his back, knocking the wind out of him, and positioned myself between his legs.

"Hold your thighs," I said as I sat on my heels. "I want you open and ready." I had nothing to bind him with, so I had to improvise. Judging by the way his pupils were blown, he liked me ordering him around. Well, he'd like what I was about to do even more.

"You look so beautiful like that, spread and hard for me," I praised as I played with his nipple, rolling the bud between my fingers before going in for a taste. Oisin arched under me, slicking our dicks together.

"You feel so good," he moaned.

"You do too, babe." I gave in, fusing our mouths together and undulating against him until we both were on the verge of climax. He whimpered when I sat up.

"Get back here." He reached for my arm.

Tasting salt and sweat, I made my way down past his torso to where his flavor was the strongest. I mouthed his cock, sliding back the foreskin, minding the curved metal ring at its tip. He kept his hips still as I sucked him, but he'd moved both his hands off his thighs and threaded his fingers in my hair. I kept going, playing with his sack, slowly moving lower to where that little captive bead ring waited at his taint. I'd seen Georgia do demonstrations with these piercings but never had the pleasure of experiencing it. I'd learned to be cautious—to gently rub it while gauging Oisin's reaction, making sure I didn't do anything that might cause pain.

"You can tug harder. Yeah, like that." He bit his lip and closed his eyes. I could play with him for hours, exploring every part of his body to learn the places that drove him crazy, the ones that made him weep, edging him until he was out of his mind.

"Please, Trent. God, I need you inside me." Instead of answering him, I pushed his legs back and grabbed a pillow to stuff under his ass, lifting it to the perfect playing height.

"Hold them...wider. There, that's it." He canted his hips, fucking the air.

"So greedy." My dick leaked, eager to get inside, but I had other plans. Spreading his cheeks, I licked a stripe down to his puckered hole, feeling the muscle contract every time I lapped him. His breath hitched when I speared his tight entrance with my tongue.

"You like that, boy?" That got him harder, just like it had the first time I'd used it with him.

"Yes, oh God, yes!"

I wet my fingers and pushed them past the ring of muscle, rousing him and making him weep with desire. "Tell me you want me to fuck you."

"Please fuck me, Sir," he panted.

I left him, spread and open, and went to my overnight bag to retrieve a special toy, along with lube and a condom.

"You brought a prostate massager?"

"Have you used one before?"

"Yeah, but I didn't have much luck. It felt too awkward doing it myself."

"This one is amazing." I hooked one of his legs on my shoulder and poured lube on his cock. "Stroke yourself. Hard. I want to see you on edge, baby."

"I love it when you get all bossy." Oisin played with his shaft, pumping it until the head was bright red, and his face contorted in pleasure. "I'm getting close." He opened his eyes when I turned the vibrator on.

"Slower now. That's it. Good boy." I nudged the massager around his hole, coaxing a long moan from him. "Feels good?"

His eyelids fluttered as he groaned. "Yeah."

Adding more lube, I rubbed the toy back and forth along his perineum, being sure to linger around the tender flesh under his balls and slick him up good.

Excitement shone in his eyes. He wanted it. "That feels so much better with you doing it."

"We haven't even gotten to the good stuff, yet." We'd fucked the night before, so he should be relaxed still. Clicking up the vibrator to a higher setting, I pushed the tip inside him, watching for signs of pain or pleasure. He clenched, tightening his face and his ass and forgetting all about his dick.

"Relax, Os." I placed a hand on his belly, soothing him with a firm touch. Immediately, he released the tension. "Bear down as I push into you."

He nodded.

The black head of the vibrator disappeared inside him. "Looks so fucking sexy." To take the full length, he'd need a distraction. I poured lube into my hand and circled Oisin's cock, pumping him with firm strokes, harder than he'd done to himself. "Keep fucking your hand," I encouraged, releasing him. "Nice and steady. That's it." Sweat broke across his forehead. Oisin tilted his head back, eyes closed, back bowed, enveloped in sensation.

*Beautiful.*

I pulled the vibrator out, moving it in circles around the tight outer ring, and then plunged it into his body, sliding it back and forth, harder and harder, as he moaned and screamed incoherent words. His cock leaked over his hand.

It was time to bring it up a notch. But not without permission, because this was not going to be a light spanking, not like the first time.

"Do you like being spanked, Oisin?"

"Yeah...I think...so."

I smacked his ass with a loud *whap*!

"Fuck! Yes!" Oisin yelled.

"Do you want another?"

"Yes!" I hit him again, pleased with the pink mark left behind.

"Yes what?" A final smack darkened the rosy shade.

"Yes, Sir. Shit, I'm so close!" His eyes were screwed shut.

"Take the handle."

"What?"

"Take the toy. I want to watch you fuck yourself with it."

"Kinky." Keeping one leg resting on my shoulder, Oisin reached down and grabbed the dildo. "You're making me do all the work." One hand on his cock, one on the toy, Oisin managed to contort his body and pump away. Watching the tip disappear and reappear was mesmerizing and so fucking hot.

"Oh shit. That's gorgeous." I gave myself a couple strokes. "Watch yourself." Through a heavy gaze, he did.

"Oh God, that's so...*fuck*. I-I'm not gonna last much longer."

Putting my hand over his, I pushed the vibrator farther into him than he'd done, aiming for his P-spot.

But it wasn't nearly enough.

"Ready for more?"

"More?" He laughed. "Yeah, I'm ready."

I clicked up the vibrator to its highest setting, fucking him as deep and as hard as I could. His hand slipped off, but I didn't care. I wanted control now. I grabbed his other leg so both ankles rested on my shoulders, granting me full access. The new position let him get lost in sensation.

"How does that feel?" His body was tense, dangling on the edge.

"Oh God! Trent!" Oisin fisted the sheets and released a sobbing moan as milky fluid leaked from his cock.

I loved hearing him scream my name more than I liked hearing him call me Sir.

"I want you to fucking come. Right. Now." I stroked his uncut beauty, matching the thrusts of the massager, giving him the touch he needed to release.

"Trent! Oh...fuck... Ngh!" he wailed as a different orgasm wrecked his body.

Fucking and milking him like that? I could do that shit all day...but not now. My own release was too near. I removed the vibrator and grabbed my rigid cock, eager to paint my lover in white. A few deft strokes and the orgasm struck, threatening to incinerate me as I shot hot streams all over Oisin's stomach and chest.

Panting, I sat back on my heels and admired the mess. "You look so fucking hot."

He glanced at his stomach and laughed. "I'm covered in jizz, and I look hot?"

"You have no idea." I ran a finger through the puddle and brought it to my mouth. Our flavors mixed well—salty, sweaty, and tangy.

"I might look hot, but you have the best face when you're fucking me, like nothing else exists. Makes me want to please you and do things like screw myself with toys and—" Oisin scooped some of the come from his belly and licked it off his fingers. "—do *that* because I know you'll get off on it."

Fuck me. I lay down on top of him and kissed the come from his mouth. This boy drove me crazy, absolutely crazy in a way that felt like my libido had been on vacation for years, and Oisin had some magical Viagra in his blood.

"How am I going to keep my hands off you in public?" I asked. The task seemed impossible. I craved him—his touch, his flesh, his affections.

Grazing his fingers along my back, he replied, "No idea. But we don't have to worry about that right now." He pressed his lips against mine with a quick kiss. "We should shower before we get stuck together."

"What's the rush?" I dragged my lips across his jaw, his morning stubble catching on my beard. Rutting against him and covered in our come, it wouldn't take long to get me hard for another round.

"No rush." He rocked his hips in time with mine. "Just thought we could get clean and then get dirty all over again."

"I like that idea." I ground into him, feeling him harden. "Can't wait to soap up your body, run my hands all over those tattoos."

"Fuck, the things you do to me, Trent."

"I've got so many things I want to do to you, boy." I wanted to explore Oisin's limits, tie him up, bring him to the edge, paddle him...maybe more, if he was into it. Being with him wasn't a chore, not like with Nic. Everything about it was new and nothing was expected. We had the potential to be balanced. Healthy. Oisin made sex fun again.

"Yeah, well, I've got so many things I want to do to you too, Sir." He sucked on the barbell in his lip. *Such a fucking turn-on.*

Before I could answer, my phone vibrated. Stopped. And then started again.

"You gonna get that?" Oisin shifted under me, trying to get me to move.

"I hadn't planned on it." But it kept buzzing mercilessly. I rolled off Oisin, and he got out of bed and grabbed the offending object.

"Here ya go," he said, handing it to me, and retreated into the bathroom.

I looked at the number and answered. "Hey Sis. Everything okay?"

"You sound a little breathless," Melissa replied. "If I interrupted something— Why the heck would you even answer your phone if you were in the middle of something, huh? That's not right. Poor Oisin."

"I wouldn't have picked up if someone had left a message instead of calling twice. So what's going on?" I did my best not to sound annoyed.

"Mom's having dinner at one o' clock today for Nina's fourth birthday, and I thought I'd remind you in case you got tied up at work."

"I couldn't forget my niece's birthday, Mel. I'll be there." I had Nina's present in the car.

"Mom also invited Oisin. You should bring him."

"Mom knows about Oisin?"

"I, uh, told her you two were dating." She raised her voice at the end, indicating she was unsure how I'd react.

"And here I thought you'd be able to keep a secret," I teased her. Telling my mother wouldn't put either of us in jeopardy, aside from giving her ammunition for the Find Trent a Husband campaign.

"She's known Oisin for a while. They met when we had the fundraiser over the summer to help people pay for their pet's medical expenses, and just sort of hit it off. He's a good person, Trent. Don't get freaked out because Mom likes him."

Knowing Mom approved of Oisin, let alone "hit it off" with him, was a revelation and a relief.

Oisin returned from the bathroom, his stomach wiped clean, and cuddled up next to me. "Tell your sister I said, 'Hi.'"

The warmth of his body soothed me. I hated the idea of being apart from him. As unhealthy as such a close attachment could be at this nascent stage of our relationship, it, along with a sister who would kill me if I didn't ask, propelled me to invite Oisin. "Would you like to go to Nina's fourth birthday party today?"

He bit down on his lip. "Really? I wouldn't be overstepping?"

"Put him on the phone," Melissa demanded, and without hesitating, I did.

"Hey Doc," Oisin greeted her. My sister's muffled voice came through and whatever she said caused him to snort. "Oh no, he treats me good. Very respectable. So it's the little lady's birthday? I'd love to come as long as I'm not in the way... And I can't wait to see my furry girl." A pause, and he nodded his head. "We'll be there." He gave the phone back to me.

"It's settled," Melissa declared. "See you both at one. It's super casual. Lots of messy painting and arts and crafts, so be prepared, Picasso."

"Will do, Sis. See you soon." I hung up and put the phone on the nightstand. "Are you sure you want to go to a kid's birthday party?"

"I don't mind." Oisin snuggled up in my arms. "I like your family, and Maggie will be there."

"Maggie?"

"My dog. Well, she will be eventually. I hope. Melissa's keeping her until I can get my life together." Oisin explained how he'd rescued the dog and that Melissa had agreed to foster her until he found an apartment that would allow a pet. "I don't know when that's going to happen, though." He frowned and seemed to retreat to the dark mood he'd been in after speaking with his father yesterday, only without the near-death experience.

"We'll work something out for you two."

His hazel eyes glimmered with affection. "Have I mentioned how much I love hearing you say we and us?"

"I like it, too. And if we don't want to be late for Nina's party, we should shower. I'm still sticky, and I can't believe you made me talk to my sister covered in come. That's just...wrong."

He snickered. "Let me make it up to you in the shower?"

"Deal."

Secretly, I adored his petulance, his immaturity. It gave him a naïveté, and I liked that I could be an anchor for him. He deserved happiness and a chance at the life he dreamed about. Even if it meant I might lose him while he went to veterinary school, it was my plan to help him succeed. As was finding a home for him and Maggie in Davis, California.

# Chapter Eighteen

Trenton

We were almost a half hour late for Nina's party. Oisin and I had to stop at two separate stores for him to buy gifts: a bouquet each for Melissa and Meredith and a present for Nina. I had a bottle of wine for them, as usual.

My sister lived in a modest suburban home, equally as void of greenery and distinction as the house where I was staying. Kids played and rode their bikes in the dead-end street, something I rarely if ever saw in West Hollywood, or LA.

Oisin fidgeted, smoothing down his jacket. "Do I look okay?"

"You look gorgeous enough to eat."

"Be sure to leave room for later, because I'm gonna stuff you." He laughed mid-sentence. "Sorry, that was so...corny."

"That *was* pretty bad." I still smiled. "And if anyone is going to be stuffed later, it'll be you."

"No switching?"

"I'll think about it." I pressed the doorbell and the ringing sent my sister's dogs in a fury, barking and clawing behind the door, followed by Mel's husband yelling at them to calm down.

"Good to see you again, Trent." My brother-in-law Gareth shook my hand and then reached for Oisin's. Their dog, Goldie, a yellow Labrador retriever, greeted me along with an unfamiliar older black dog with strands of white fur around its muzzle and eyes.

"Maggie!" Oisin beamed and immediately dropped down to the dog's level, scratching her neck and hugging her. "How are you, girl?" She wagged her stocky tail while Goldie wedged her way between them.

Gareth scratched the back of his head. "Meet Maggie, Oisin's stray. We're just keeping her until we find her proper owners or until he can take her."

"You're looking good, girl." Oisin examined her leg and stomach, both of which had new fur growing in.

"What happened?" I asked.

Oisin gave her another pat and stood up. "She had a broken leg and a tumor in her stomach. Thankfully, it was benign." His passion and love for Maggie radiated in the tender way he looked at her and the gentle pats he absentmindedly gave her as he spoke.

"You certainly do love animals."

He lowered his head and nuzzled Maggie. "They're the best. And this gal's got my heart, that's for sure." He put his hand under her chin and lifted it. "Just look at those brown eyes. Aren't they sweet?" The dog moved her head and licked at his fingers, clearly loving all the affection.

"Look at you two!" Melissa entered the hallway and greeted us with a broad smile and hugs. "Mom is going to be so happy. Come in."

"Is that who I think it is?" Meredith, holding her sleeping one-year-old son, approached us with her mouth open in disbelief. "Holy sh—shoot! When did this happen?"

"Blame Melissa and her matchmaking skills," I replied.

She narrowed her eyes at her twin. "I cannot believe you kept this all to yourself!"

"If you'd come in to work and not lounge around taking care of Kevin, you'd have been up on all the gossip."

"Sure, if you want to stay up all night with this rug rat, I'd be more than happy to go into the office. He's getting a new tooth and he's not so happy about it."

"Ouch."

"See? I win. Anyway, how long have you two been dating?"

"They just hooked up Monday," Melissa answered before I could.

"And now you're meeting the family together? Brave. *Very brave.*"

"Who's this little guy?" Oisin asked as he gently touched my nephew's arm.

"This is Kevin. He's thirteen months tomorrow." The baby must have known someone was talking about him because he yawned and stretched, opening his blue eyes to look around. "Wanna hold him?"

"Gimme!" Oisin lit up and reached for Kevin. Within seconds, Oisin was rocking my nephew and rubbing his tiny chin, as baby fingers wrapped around his pinky. "I think I'm in love." Apparently, Kevin didn't feel quite the same way. He started to holler, and then squished up his face—a telltale sign that he was about to pass some gas. "Whoa!" Oisin laughed. "Dang, little guy. Here, I think that's your cue." He passed Kevin back to Meredith, who was laughing hard. "Gotta stop feeding him baked beans, Dr. Martin."

"Oh man," she said, taking a whiff of her baby. "Yeah. It's time for a change. Excuse me." She disappeared with Kevin into a side room.

"I'm so glad Nina is potty trained," Melissa chimed in. "Come on, let's go see everyone."

We followed her and Gareth into a living room full of chaos, where music played and children laughed while making various crafts with their adults. When Nina, who was painting something with my mother, saw me, she dropped the paintbrush and ran over with her arms open. Mom trailed behind her.

"Uncle T! You're here!" Nina smashed into my legs and grabbed them in a hug.

"Hey, munchkin." I knelt down and hugged her once she'd finished accosting my legs. "Do you remember Oisin?"

She nodded, instantly turning shy and mute.

"She likes him," my sister informed me.

"Runs in the family."

"There you are," Mom said. I rose, and she hugged us and gave us each a little peck on the cheek. Holding one of my hands and one of Oisin's, she looked at us with an expression that radiated pure joy. "I was wondering when you were going to get here." She had rosy cheeks and a fair complexion, and we shared the same eye color, although hers shone with more tenderness than mine ever had. "I'm so happy for the two of you." She gave my hand a squeeze before letting go.

Oisin bit down on his lip as he looked to me.

"No pressure there, Mom," I teased. "It's all very new and hush-hush for now."

"Oh? Why's that?" She frowned. "Are you in the closet, honey?" she asked Oisin. "I thought you said you were out."

"No." Oisin laughed nervously. "No closet here. My dad is Trent's boss, so it makes things a little tricky."

"My son is a good man. I don't see why your father would have any problems with the two of you together. But what does this old lady know?" She shrugged. "Your secret's safe with me."

Nina tugged at Melissa's pant leg and motioned for her to come down to munchkin height to whisper in her ear.

"I'll ask him, but he might say no, okay?" Melissa replied. "Os, she wants to know if you'll help her paint something."

Oisin placed a hand to his chest. "I would be honored, ladybug." He sent me a smile and said, "I'll see you after we create a masterpiece."

The two of them left hand in hand for the craft station where Nina and my mother had been when we arrived. Oisin appeared perfectly at home with my family, like he'd always belonged here. The sight caused an unexpected fullness in my heart.

"You've got it bad for that one." My mother rubbed my arm, a gesture of comfort she'd done since I was little. "I can see why. He's got such a sweet soul." Mom had never been close to Nic, who was mostly distant and awkward whenever he and I visited. So her voiced approval of Oisin had been unexpected.

"He's so much younger than me, and he acts it, too." The meltdown in the car was a perfect example. "As I said, we just started dating, so I don't want you to get your hopes up just yet. No picking out silverware, okay?" I was joking—she'd never do anything like that.

"Dang it. I had the perfect pattern, too." She let out a soft laugh.

My sister and Gareth introduced me to the other guests, who were parents of the rug rats mostly. After meeting everyone, I went over to where Nina and Oisin—with his faithful black Lab by his side—were hard at work on their paintings. Nina had decided to paint on Oisin's face.

He turned to me with the biggest smile and a long blue streak on his nose. "Is it me? I'm not sure if this is the right shade."

Nina giggled in delight.

"Definitely your shade."

"Good. I was worried." He continued painting with Nina, dodging her artistic attempts to paint his face with alternate colors.

I picked up a colored pencil and some paper from the craft table and sketched a caricature of Oisin and Nina while they continued to paint. It'd been too long since I'd drawn anything, and I found joy in the familiarity of the motions.

"That looks like a finished masterpiece to me," Oisin proudly said to Nina, who held her artwork up with paint-covered hands. "You should let your mom see your brilliant work." Nina ran off to show the painting. He grabbed a paper towel from the table and tried to wipe the paint off his face, missing some. He came over to where I was sitting and looked down at the sketch. "That's really good. I didn't know you could draw."

"I minored in art in college. I used to do it more when I was a kid." The sketch had come out better than I expected considering my absence from the craft.

"I love it."

"Then keep it." I handed it to him.

"It's so cute. I didn't know my lips were that pouty or Nina's nose was that big."

"It's true to life," I gibed. The cartoon drawing exaggerated features, as any caricature portrait would.

"Hmm. Well, all the better to kiss you then." And he did, softly and sweetly, rubbing his nose against mine before pulling away.

"You got me, didn't you?"

He grinned. "Yep. Blue is a good color on you."

I found myself mirroring his wide smile. This fun-loving side of him was exactly what I needed to lighten up. I reached into a pod of paint, and with my fingers covered in yellow, ran a streak down his cheek. "Yellow suits you better, I think."

"You had to go there." He got a pod of red paint and dumped it on his hand. I dodged just as he went to rub it in my face, and he hit the back of my head instead. The wetness seeped to my scalp.

"We still have to eat cake and open presents with Nina." I avoided another handful of paint—blue this time.

"And?" He tried to get ahold of me, blue paint running from his hand and down his wrist.

"And now we're Technicolor guests." I grabbed the rest of the yellow paint and dumped it on his head, sending a few four-year-olds laughing and screaming for their moms.

While I gloated in my temporary triumph, Oisin turned away and made as if he was getting a towel off the craft table. Within seconds, I found myself smothered in blue. He'd gotten me again. I must have looked like a Smurf.

"Boys?" My mom, who'd been helping Melissa in the kitchen, returned with a couple of the children we'd sent running earlier. "What are you two doing?" She chuckled.

"Painting," I replied, wiping the stuff off my lips. "Unconventionally." That sent Oisin into a peal of laughter.

"I see. Well, you best get cleaned up quick. It's time for presents and cake."

I wiped my face with the paper towel Oisin handed me. "Okay, thank you." I couldn't remember the last time I'd seen my mother look at me with that much warmth and happiness.

Crinkles formed around her eyes in amusement. "I think Melissa keeps her towels in the hallway closet upstairs."

I waggled my eyebrows at Oisin.

"We are not going to do anything in your sister's house." Oisin swatted me in the chest, splotching more paint on my shirt. "Oops, sorry."

I lowered my voice so he alone could hear. "This coming from someone who made me talk to my sister while covered in come and gave me a blow job on the highway at seventy-five miles per hour."

He flushed. "Not the same thing."

"And here I thought you were the adventurous one. Come on." I led us up the stairs, picking up a couple washcloths and towels from the closet before going into the bathroom. We kept it a sex-free zone as we washed the paint off. Being water based, it came off with ease.

"Stay with me tonight," I said as I wiped away some lingering yellow paint off Oisin's ear.

"Really? You're not sick of me, yet?"

"No, babe. I don't think I'll ever be sick of you." I kissed his neck. "Of your taste." I grazed my lips along his neck, feeling the stubble prickle my lips. "Or your scent." I nipped at his ear. "Or being in that tight little hole of yours." I grabbed a handful of his pert ass for emphasis.

He groaned my name, sounding somewhere between pleasure and annoyance.

"Don't worry. I'll save it all for later." I kissed his lips and opened the bathroom door, leaving him behind as I returned to the party below. I had no doubt he'd be spending the night with me.

# Chapter Nineteen

OISIN

My mother's real estate office was located in Summerlin, a few minutes' drive from my childhood home. I'd brought her lunch, a Greek salad and a side of hummus, her favorite, since she said her schedule was too busy to meet me somewhere today.

When she greeted me, she looked as meticulous as usual, not a hair out of place. I thought she might be less than put together considering the pending divorce, but I supposed she was too professional to show that side of herself at work.

"Thank you. You're such a sweet kid," she said when I handed her the bag. She motioned for me to follow her to her corner office.

"Do you want some of this?" She sat down behind her desk and removed the contents of the bag.

"No thanks," I said and took a seat opposite her. "I ate before I got here." I was too nervous to eat anything.

"So what brings you by? I don't usually get a visit."

"I got a call from Dad's lawyer today."

She set her fork down. "Why would his lawyer call you?"

"To let me know that until I decide to return to law school full-time, I'm surviving on five hundred a month until my thirtieth birthday, and that I owe him this year's tuition."

"He messed with your trust? *We* set that up for you. He had no right!" Mom clenched her jaw. "I can't believe him, or that he didn't even have the decency to call you himself."

I hated that I'd made her so angry, but I wouldn't be able to pay for my apartment, let alone food, if I didn't find some work.

"I wish I could give you the money, but our assets are frozen until the divorce is finalized."

We were supposed to be a family, not taking sides like we were fighting a war. Going to my mother and telling her what Dad had done was giving her more ammunition to hate him. I wished I could've left her out of it, but continuing with my law degree was emotional suicide.

"I was hoping you might know someone who'd hire me part time while I finish out the semester?" It'd been three weeks since Dad said he'd cut off my trust, but I thought he'd reconsidered since he hadn't sent the papers over. I didn't have enough in my account to pay rent because, in spite of Melissa's protest, I'd spent my reserves on Maggie's vet bills.

"I could use your help around the office, if you don't mind working for me. And if you need a place to stay, you can move back home. I'd like the company, to be honest. That place is too big now that you boys are all grown up."

"Thanks, Mom. I'll probably have to take you up on that offer." My father had been the one who'd insisted I move out my freshman year of college, something I probably would've done even if I wasn't forced out of the nest.

She dipped a pita slice into the hummus and ate it, clearly fuming about what my dad had done. When she finished, she pushed the food aside, and I knew this convo was about to get personal.

"It's been a while since we talked. Do you want to tell me why you were having a hard time with school?"

"I don't want to be a lawyer."

"Thank God." She laughed. "Forgive me, but I just couldn't picture you doing what your father does."

"What did you see me doing?"

"Before you met Carrie, all you talked about was becoming a vet, so I thought that's what you were going to do."

"It is. I applied to UC Davis and got in. I've applied for loans and work-study, but I don't think I'll have enough for tuition."

"You got in? Oh, honey! I'm so happy for you!" She got up from her desk and gave me a hug. Taking my face in her hands she said, "I've been so worried. And here you are, making all these wonderful plans for your future. I'm so proud of you."

"Thanks."

"When I talk to my attorney, I'll see what we can do about tuition. There's no reason why your father shouldn't pay for it, or at least let you pay for it with the money we set aside." She huffed. "Never marry a lawyer."

*What if I was already falling for one?*

"Now, what else is going on with you? Are you seeing anyone?"

"Sort of." I couldn't lie to my mother. "But we have to keep it secret for now."

"Can you tell me her name at least?"

"It's a *he*, and no. I wish I could but—"

"Oh."

"Oh?"

"It's nothing, honey." She sat at her desk and starting organizing the already neat surface.

"Mom?"

"I'm sorry. I don't mean to sound upset. I'm not. I just thought— It doesn't matter. Does he treat you well?"

"Yes. And he's all for me going into veterinary medicine." I tried not to let my disappointment show. I thought my mother, a PFLAG member, understood me and didn't care what gender I fell in love with as long as I was happy. That was what she used to tell me anyway.

"Then I like him already." Her face softened. Maybe she only needed a moment to adjust to the idea of me being with a man, rather than outright disapproving it.

"I should let you get back to work." I stood and walked around her desk to give her a hug.

"You can always come to me, Os," she said as we embraced.

"I can start working tomorrow if that's okay?" I asked, letting her go.

"I'll be here at nine."

"And I appreciate you letting me live back home. I'm going to ask Devon if I can stay with him first."

"All right, honey. The door's always open, so whenever you want to come home, you can."

I went back to my apartment feeling slightly better that my mother was on my side.


I TAPED UP the bottom of a box and went into the bedroom to pack the set of extra sheets and blankets, figuring I could do without them until the end of the week when I had to move.

"Knock, knock." Devon tapped on the bedroom door.

I jumped and dropped the sheets, laughing when I realized it was my best friend. "You scared me."

"You must have been in deep thought because I texted and knocked on your front door—the doorbell is busted. I used the key to get in." He gave me a warm hug, infusing my senses with his familiar vanilla scent. "Your dad cut you off, huh?"

"Yup."

"I'm sorry, Os." Devon squeezed my hand.

"Since he and Mom split up, he's become a dick. I can't talk to him anymore." Dad had been a hero to me growing up. Even in high school, when he was in LA more than home, my father represented Devon, navigating my friend through the process of becoming an emancipated minor. Those things made me want to be like him, to be able to give back to those who needed assistance.

"The good part about all of this is I don't have to go to shrink appointments, or tutors, or live up to his expectations." I may have lost the majority of my father's respect and financial support, but instead of feeling like a failure, it was like I was finally moving toward something positive. Veterinary school was more a reality than a dream, as long as I could get the tuition money.

"Your mom couldn't help you with the rent?"

"The lawyers have her accounts all tied up until my parents go through their assets. She's on a strict budget until the divorce is finalized, and that could take a year or more." Dad was an asshole for cheating on mom and deserved nothing.

"I can't believe they're really divorcing." Devon had been shocked by the news of my father's indiscretions as much as I had.

"Me neither." I fidgeted, knowing I was about to impose upon my BFF. "I was kinda hoping I could stay with you until I found another place."

"Um, actually, I have some news," he said and picked up the sheets I'd dropped and handed them to me. "I took your advice and proposed that Stone's band record some of their songs here in Vegas."

"And?"

"And starting next week, they are!" Devon clapped.

"That's huge! Congratulations! So you worked everything out?"

"Stone said he'd be pissed if I turned down the gig at Charlie's garage because of him, and he doesn't want to give up on us." He glowed with happiness.

"But what about never seeing him because of touring and the paparazzi?"

"There's not much he can do about that. It goes with the gig. I just—"

That lovesick glaze passed over his eyes, and I knew what was coming. "You just love him too much."

"I just love him." My friend gave a dimpled smile. "I have to make this work, Os."

"You will. You are. I'm so happy for you!" Devon deserved all the love he could get. While I suspected Stone wouldn't have a problem bending for Dev, I was worried his career would be less flexible since it involved his band members, too.

Devon sat on my bed. "What about you and Trent? I take it you've stayed on the down-low successfully."

"For now, possibly for good." I wasn't sure how Devon would take the news of my future plans, and I figured it would be best to just come out and say it. "I'm planning on moving to California for veterinary school in September."

"That's great!" He sprung off the bed and hugged me. "You're finally doing it!"

I exhaled, relieved that Dev was so enthusiastic. "Thanks."

"But what's that got to do with you not telling your dad about Trent?" He twisted his lips and looked perplexed.

"There's no point if Trent and I aren't together. He'll be too busy with work and I'll be too busy with school in a few months."

"So, you're gonna break up with him because he's living here and you'll be in California?"

"I don't see an alternative."

He folded his arms and stared at me. "That's bullshit." Devon hardly swore, making the impact more dramatic.

"It's not bullshit. We'll be living in two states, living two different lives, and I won't have the money or time to visit every weekend, not like you and Stone. I can't stay here for him, Dev. I did that for Carrie and it made me miserable."

"You're afraid, Os. You're so scared about being in love with Trent, you'd rather run away than stick through the hard stuff."

"He and I have been together a few weeks. It's too early to say if I'm in love with him or if he's in love with me."

"You can be such a hypocrite sometimes."

I recoiled. "What do you mean?"

"You were all gung ho, talking about how Stone and I loved each other when we started our long-distance romance. Why should you and Trent be any different? At least you've lived in the same state for the entire time you've dated, and you've got until August or September to figure it all out. It's not like Trent tours the globe and has hot men and women throwing themselves at him like Stone does." He huffed dramatically and waved. "You two got it easy-peasy as far as I'm concerned."

Devon had a point. I just couldn't admit that I was scared. I liked this chapter of my life with Trent and wanted to preserve it, not risk it being torn apart like what had happened with my parents' relationship or my relationship with Carrie.

I wrapped my arm around my waist, comforting myself. "It's only been three weeks," I mumbled. Three short weeks and I already couldn't imagine Trent not being in my life without my chest tightening.

"I knew Stone less than a month, same as you, before that crazy singer decided to rent a place here and date me. Have a little faith, Os. You know how you're always making fun of the way I look when I talk about Stone, all lovey-dovey and dream-like? Well, my friend, you get that same look when you're talking about Trent. Own it. Take the risk. That's what you told me."

"I give some whacky advice."

He chuckled. "Your whacky advice was good advice."

I stuffed the sheets into the box and scanned the room, looking for anything else I could manage a week without. A picture of Maggie and me rested on my nightstand. I loved that stinky mutt and planned on renting a place that accepted big dogs after I finished this lease. Living with Melissa's family, she had the love of Nina and the company of their dog, Goldie. I wondered if she'd be happier staying where she was.

As if Devon read my thoughts, he asked, "Are you going to take Maggie?"

"I don't think I'd be able to spend enough time with her between work and school."

"You'll make it work."

"Yeah, probably." I shrugged. "One crisis at a time. I have to figure out where I'm going to live."

"I could stay with Stone at his apartment until you find a place," Devon offered. The apartment Stone had rented back in November when they'd first started dating was upscale from what Devon told me, but forcing my friend out of his home seemed unfair.

"You guys aren't planning to move into your place together while he's here?"

"We're going to live together while he's here but haven't decided where. My place would be easier but it's smaller and with the restaurant downstairs, there's always a crowd around. I think his place would be safer and better for the both of us. He's coming here the end of the week, so you won't be kicking me out of my home. You'll just have to help me pack." Devon forced a smile, and I knew he didn't really want to move out of the condo he'd made his home. Sooner or later he'd have to decide where Stone and he would live, but I wasn't going to force him one way or the other, not when I had another option.

"You could ask Trent."

"And stay at the house the company pays for?"

"Poetic justice, I'd say. Besides, there's probably like four unused bedrooms in the place—not that you'd be sleeping in separate beds or anything."

It'd be nice to wake up next to Trent every day, but it'd make it that much harder to leave him when school started. "Mom said I could crash with her, so I'll probably go there."

"Suit yourself. Not as much lovin' lovin' for you...or morning nookie. I know how much you like morning nookie."

Yup, I was blushing. I could feel the heat rise from my toes to my face.

"Do you want some help packing?"

"Sure. Not gonna turn down free help."

Devon left after we'd packed most of my belongings, and I realized I had less than an hour to get ready to meet Trent. We were getting together locally, which meant this fell under the guise of studying and would be a hands-off date. I hated that, but we'd been lucky that word hadn't spread about us seeing each other, especially after being spotted by both Mrs. Bryant and Carrie.

I gathered up my computer and assignments to make the date look as official as I could, and left.

The restaurant, an upscale pizza place, lacked the romantic vibe and views of the first place we'd had dinner together. Booths lined the walls and standalone tables were in the center covered with red paper tablecloths. The Venice themed décor consisted of framed paintings of the canals and gondoliers.

"They have the best pepperoni pizza, and I've had a craving all day." Trent set the menu aside without looking at it. "Someone at work brought in a few pies this week," he added.

"I think I'll get the pasta primavera."

"I can get a vegetarian pizza, if you'd prefer." Trent's mindfulness warmed me.

"I'm not standing in the way of you and your pepperoni pizza craving, but thanks for the offer."

Our order came quickly, and we ate, keeping the conversation focused on Trent's work. He'd finalized a contract he'd been negotiating for the past two weeks for a high-maintenance sports figure. His client had recently become a top player in the NBA, and according to Trent, he'd turned into a prima donna with the news.

"I've been his attorney for years, and he's not that bad of a guy, really. I shouldn't speak so harshly of him," Trent backtracked. "We negotiated a portion of his earnings to go to a college fund for intercity kids."

"Somehow, I think you influenced him into making that decision."

"I admit, seeing a certain someone fulfill his doctoral dream is one of my priorities." He took a sip of his soda. "How did your visit with your mom go? Was she able to help you?"

"No. It's like you said. Her assets are frozen until they divvy them up. I'm going to live with her until I can save up enough to move."

Trent pushed aside his dish and leaned forward. "I've been thinking about something."

"Uh-oh. This sounds serious," I teased and mirrored him, resting my arms on the table.

The smile I waited for never came. He shifted his gaze away and cleared his throat. Whatever he was about to say had weight behind it.

"I'm tired of being secretive. I want a future with you, and I think you want the same. I think we should tell your father we're dating."

"W-What?" I hadn't expected this, not after telling him I'd be saving up money for moving.

He frowned. "Do you not want to be together?"

"No, it's not that. I-I just think it's too soon to say anything. Why not wait until after you make junior partner?" My question caused that tiny vein in his forehead to appear. I'd upset him.

"Because I'm falling in love with you and keeping quiet about it is too much like being closeted and ashamed." Trent's eyes widened. "Shit. I didn't mean to say it. I mean, I didn't mean to blurt it out like that." He ran a hand through his hair. "I'm digging myself deeper, aren't I?"

Stunned, I stared at Trent completely terrified of what he was proposing. If I admitted my feelings, I knew I'd want to stay in Vegas to be with him, like I'd done with Carrie. I couldn't risk losing my one chance of breaking free. And then there was Trent's career. It didn't matter if Trent stayed in Vegas or moved to Davis with me, he'd be giving up his promotion, something he'd ultimately resent me for later on. I'd been ignoring that issue. Telling my father about us would only screw up Trent's life and mine.

There was no future for us if we both wanted to pursue our passions.

Feeling nauseous, I stood and pulled some cash out of my wallet, not paying attention at how much I tossed on the table. "I should go. I have to move my things to my mother's house, and..." I turned and left the restaurant, clutching my stomach as my nerves threaten to purge veggie pizza.

I inhaled deeply when I got outside and walked to my car, my head down. "Fuck, fuck, fuck." A million questions raced in my mind, each one turning on itself about how Trent and I could possibly have a future for all the reasons I'd mentioned to Devon earlier. I'd have to face the coming months without Trent because staying and knowing he was in love with me would ruin the will I had to move to California. The past was something I couldn't repeat, no matter how much I cared for and quite possibly, no, *did* love him.

I wasn't paying attention to where I was walking and bumped into someone. "Sorry." I didn't bother looking up until I heard his familiar voice.

"You should watch where you're going," Kyle warned. A member of his ass hat posse, the one who'd cheered him on as he kicked my ribs after I blew him, was with him.

"Fuck off, Kyle." I turned around and kept walking, not caring what he or his flying monkey might do.

I'd made it to my car before I heard Trent yelling at me to stop. Reluctantly, I faced him, taking a quick scan of the area and spotting Kyle and his friend by the front door of the restaurant. *Great. An audience.*

"I get that you're younger than me," Trent fumed, "but running away instead of having a calm discussion about our relationship is infantile."

My insides quaked, torn between the dream I'd given up on and the man who'd come to mean far more than I'd anticipated. I'd made the wrong choice in the past, and I couldn't—wouldn't—do it again. Not for love. "We shouldn't see each other again." I clicked the key fob to my car and got inside, shutting the door as quickly as I could.

He pounded on the window, blue eyes blazing. "Dammit, Oisin, that's not fair, and you know it."

I drove away, trying to convince myself I'd done the right thing by ending our relationship and that the ache in my heart was from the acidic pizza sauce, not from heartbreak.

# Chapter Twenty

TRENTON

Harrison and I had exchanged several emails since our last conversation, all of which were work related. Nothing about Oisin. At all. In the email I sent last week, I informed Harrison that his son was doing well in his contracts class. The return email focused on an upcoming interview for a law clerk position at this branch. He implied it was mere courtesy, a favor he owed to a colleague, and the fresh-out-of-law-school graduate lacked the qualifications he required from his clerks. There was no mention of Oisin.

"He still hasn't called you back?" my matchmaking sister asked when I called her for moral support.

"No, and he hasn't returned my texts." It'd been a week since we'd last seen each other, three days since my last message to him, and I'd heard nothing. I assumed he would've calmed down and contacted me by now. "Has he been to the clinic?"

"No, we haven't seen him this week. I thought he was busy spending time with you."

"I'm an idiot, Mel. I shouldn't have blurted out that I was in love with him." I had to admit, though, that I was relieved to get my feelings out there.

"He'll come around. From the way he looks when he talks about you, I'd say he's got it bad. Hang in there."

"He's leaving for UC Davis in August, that gives me until then to work everything out." My family hadn't been happy to learn I planned on returning to California. I explained I was ready to start living life, taking long vacations, and enjoying the ocean instead of being chained to a desk in a smog-filled city. California was my home, and when I thought about my future, Oisin was with me, basking in the rays by the Pacific.

"I can't believe after all this you're moving back to the Golden State. We're going to miss you."

"I promise to visit more this time."

"Uh-huh. I know you, little brother, and you got a workaholic streak a mile wide." A muffled voice in the background spoke to my sister. "Okay, I'll be there in a second. Trent, I've to get back to work. See you this weekend?"

"You bet."

Jana lightly knocked on my open office door. "Mr. Fisher, Kyle Hernandez is here to see you."

I suppressed a groan. I had no time for this damn interview. Two contracts needed to be finalized and out to our clients by the end of the day. Jana was drafting the second contract while I ensured all the negotiated points were met on the first. We were slightly behind schedule, which meant I needed to get this guy out of here as quickly as I could. "Send him in."

A slender young man about Oisin's age entered my office with a confident stride. He had a large nose that leaped out from his oblong face and wore an expensive pinstriped suit. The pretentiousness floating around him made me want to smack that smug clean-shaven face.

"Thank you for taking the time to meet with me, Mr. Fisher." He proffered his hand and met mine with a firm shake. "I've brought a copy of my qualifications and letters of recommendations from my professors as well as past employers."

I took the documents, the same ones Harrison had forwarded to me via email, and pretended to review them. "These are impressive." In fact, the resume and recommendations were mediocre, as if he'd skated along and only did what was required. There was no volunteer work and nothing in the documentation that spoke of having passion for the field. I knew this firm well enough to recognize that every single employee, whether an attorney, clerk, or paralegal, had a fervor for the legal field. It had drawn me to Harrison, Preston, and Bryant, Inc. long before I graduated from law school.

"Thank you," he said, squaring his shoulders and preening at the compliment as I knew he would.

I sat on the corner of my desk and motioned him to the chair facing me. "But I've seen better, more qualified law students who've attended better universities. What is it that sets you apart from them?"

He tilted his chin up. "You'll find me meticulous, professional, and—"

"Come on, do better than that. Give me something original." I knew I was being a prick, but the truth was this kid wasn't that special. There *were* better candidates for the law clerk position, ones without the arrogance.

"I see. I was under the impression this interview was a formality." He crossed his legs. "Did Mr. Harrison not inform you that he owed my father a favor and in turn he'd hire me?"

Not only did this kid act superior, he thought it was his God-given right to be here, and it pissed me off.

"And you'd be perfectly content gaining employment based on a favor rather than your own merits?" I'd known plenty of people who used their connections to advance their careers, including me. However, being hired as a consequence of an owed favor without the proper qualifications bypassed all self-respect. And Harrison had given no indication he intended to hire the little shit.

Sitting back in his chair and folding his hands, he said, "I see nothing wrong with getting a foot in the door where I can."

"Well, Mr. Hernandez, I can assure you there is nothing wrong with getting a foot in the door, but acting as if you're entitled may earn you a foot in the ass. I suggest you rethink your approach."

He stood up and smoothed down his suit jacket. "When my father hears about how I've been treated, I'm sure he'll inform your boss and let him know how unprofessional you've been."

"You do that, and you'll see just how much everyone loves a tattletale." I stayed glued to my desk and folded my arms, staring the fucker down. I couldn't wait for the kid to leave so I could get some real work done.

He made it to the doorway before turning around. "Oh, one more thing, Mr. Fisher. Does your boss know you're fucking his son? Not that I can blame you. Everybody knows he gives excellent head. I know firsthand, as do several of my classmates."

The image of Oisin down on his knees sucking on that vile piece of garbage's dick turned my stomach. Kyle seemed like a wild card—someone who'd fabricate anything to get what he wanted. More than likely, he'd lied about Oisin... *But Oisin does give excellent head. Fucker!*

I clenched my fists, using all my restraint not to punch the twat. "I suggest you leave before I call security."

"No need." He rapped on the doorjamb twice. "Have a good night."

I let my shoulders drop. This week absolutely sucked.

As I moved behind my desk, I stared down at the contract. Kyle may or may not have found a way to plant an earworm in Harrison's business circle. If he was the type of sanctimonious jackass to do it, which seemed more likely than not, it'd be better to approach my boss about my relationship with Oisin before the twat put a negative spin on it. The problem was, Oisin disapproved of the idea, wholeheartedly, and he'd ended our relationship over it. There might be nothing left to admit. Then again, should Kyle manage to attract Harrison's attention, Harrison believed his son to be promiscuous and would likely believe the snotty kid. Harrison may not be the best advocate of honesty, given he'd cheated on his wife, but he'd been a mentor and instrumental to my success as an attorney. If there were any chance for Oisin and me to be together, clearing the air with my boss would be necessary.

I found Harrison in my contacts and tapped SEND. Anxiety pulsed through my veins and made my insides queasy at the sound of the ringing on the other end.

"Fisher, if you've called to talk about Kyle's behavior, save your breath. I already know the kid's an ass and so does his father." Harrison chuckled.

"That's actually good to hear, sir, but if you have a moment, I'd like to talk to you about Oisin."

"Go on." The change in his lighthearted mood reached through the phone.

Suddenly, it was as if I'd swallowed shards of glass. The thought of denying whatever Kyle thought he'd seen or whatever rumor he'd started sounded more appealing. None of it would lift the burden of lying to my boss. None of it would give Oisin and me a chance to make amends and date freely. Regardless of how this conversation went, I'd try to contact Oisin again and prove that I loved him for who he was and would continue to encourage him to follow his dreams.

Risking the honest approach once more I uttered, "Oisin and I have been seeing each other romantically."

Harrison took a long pause before responding, "I ask you to mentor him, to treat him like a brother, and you're saying you've been screwing him? Oisin doesn't need you, or anyone, messing with his head right now. He's not well. What he needs is guidance, not someone to be his leather daddy."

A chill ran down my spine. Harrison couldn't know about what Nic and I did. We were discreet. I brushed off the comment as best I could. "I met him in Los Angeles before you asked me to mentor him, and even then I didn't know the person I was with was Oisin. He looked different."

"Let me guess," Harrison replied, adding an audible sigh. "He was in drag when you met him. That boy. If it weren't for Devon, my son would've stayed a man and never have gotten into cross-dressing. As much as I love Devon like a son, I wish he hadn't influenced my boy so much."

I remained silent. Oisin liked wearing feminine things, the underwear in particular, and that was definitely something his father would be better off not knowing, but that did not make him less of a man.

"Trenton, I say this as Oisin's father, not your boss. There were rumors about your previous relationship, and while I'm not one to pay attention to them, they implied you lived a certain lifestyle. Normally, what you do in your free time doesn't matter to me, but when it comes to my son, I care, and would rather he not be involved. He's too naïve, too much a people pleaser, and I don't think he understands the psychological impact it'll have on him later in life."

I thought back to all the company parties and get-togethers Nic and I had attended, trying to figure out when rumors could have started. We'd been a part of the firm for years, and at no time did we mention what we did together in the bedroom—to anyone in LA. Ever. Or at least I hadn't. I felt violated and pissed, and wanted to hurt whomever had started those rumors.

"Oisin is a grown man, and who he should and shouldn't be with is entirely his decision. Furthermore, what I do in my private life is none of your concern. You've crossed a line, Harrison."

"When my son starts acting like an adult, I'll treat him as such." He scoffed. "You've known him how long? A few weeks? I know that boy. He'll screw anyone who gives him a speck of attention. Don't think you're special, Fisher. That day in my office, he had a hangover and had been sticking his dick where it didn't belong. He's playing you. He needs help."

What happened to the parent who was concerned about the welfare of his child? I couldn't believe he'd basically called his kid a slut. Just like Kyle had done. They were wrong. Oisin was a petulant brat at times, and sure, he gave a mean blow job, but he was incapable of being a player, and he certainly didn't stick his dick where it didn't belong.

*Gears clicked.* Oisin had confessed to getting wasted and being beaten up by a group of guys. Had Kyle been part of that group?

"You're right about one thing. Oisin needs your help. Did you know he went to law school to please you even though his heart is in veterinary medicine? That he's been accepted into the program at UC Davis and could start in September? Oisin knows what he wants." I couldn't help the heat in my voice. "The last conversation you and I had about him, you said the two of you fight whenever you try to talk, so try listening for a change. He's a good person, and—"

"Your services are no longer needed in Vegas," he barked. "The company will pay for your transfer back to California. Your old office will be available by the end of next week. One more thing—until you have children of your own, I suggest you keep your judgment and opinions to yourself." He hung up before I could reply. Obviously, I'd hit a nerve.

Oisin had more of his father's temperament than I'd realized. Best get the last word in and hang up, or in Oisin's case, run away. Like father, like son. Harrison was being petty, a lion with a thorn in his paw.

My plan was to take the transfer—maybe stay at the firm a month or two before moving to another firm that had been after me. I'd had plenty of offers over the years.

I wanted to speak with Oisin before leaving. *Unlikely.* He'd refused to answer his phone, refused to talk to me like a level-headed person. Maybe once he saw my gift to him, he'd reconsider. If not, at least I'd have done the best I could to make his dream come true.

# Chapter Twenty-One

T**RENTON**

The waiting area of Paws for Love consisted of one extremely vocal cat and her pet parent, an elderly lady. Another earsplitting meow rang out from the cat carrier and echoed off the tiled floor. *Ouch.* The woman shook her head and said, "Princess hates the vet. She'll be completely quiet on the ride home." She stuck her fingers in the carrier as the cat continued howling like its death was around the corner.

"Princess is all set in room two, Angie. Dr. Martin will be there in a moment." Melissa went to pick up the cat carrier, but the woman shooed her away.

"I got this, dear." She hefted the carrier, flexing a wrinkled bicep, proving she was stronger and less frail than I'd thought. "Weights and yoga, the key to old age," she said as she went into the exam room with her cat. Melissa shut the door, leaving the woman and Princess to the mercy of her twin.

I rubbed my ear. "Is that cat okay? I've never heard anything like that before." The animal's decibel level was on par with the volume at a Mutant Militia concert.

"She's fine. She's here for a nail trim." Melissa folded her arms, giving me the once over. "You look tired, bro. Your young'un keeping you awake at night?"

"I wish."

"What do you mean, 'You wish'?" She held up a finger. "Hold that thought." Melissa went to the reception desk where a large gift basket filled with cookies, fruit, and a bag of chocolate covered pretzels sat. "I had no time for lunch today. I'm starving. A client thanked us for saving her dog. He swallowed a toy—the dog, not the client—and it got all wrapped up in his intestines. He was constip... Never mind." She plucked out the bag of chocolate pretzels. "These are mine, but everything else is up for grabs." Melissa tore into the bag and popped a chocolate covered pretzel in her mouth. "Okay, now I can focus. What's this business about you not being with Oisin? Didn't you kiss and make up after that fight?"

"No. He won't return my calls or texts. I was hoping he'd be here."

She chomped down another pretzel before answering. "I haven't heard from him, which is a shame because I have good news. My former advisor at UC Davis said she's willing to let Oisin do work-study with her his first semester, and if that goes well, she'll approve him for the second semester. It won't be enough money to cover his tuition, but it's a start." She went behind the reception desk, prized pretzels in hand, and pulled out a sheet of paper with the university's logo from the drawer. "This is for him. He just needs to fill out the forms."

I took it from her and read it. "This is great news." I handed the paper back.

"Does he know you're moving back to Cali?"

"No idea. I got the transfer, by the way, only not quite the way I intended."

I told Melissa about the interview and the conversation with Harrison that had followed, including the rumors about my lifestyle with Nic. The subject matter of the rumors weren't a surprise to her. She knew what I was into because soon after breaking up with Nic, I'd told her the truth. I'd worried that she'd be disgusted or think I was crazy, since most people didn't understand the BDSM dynamic, but instead of judging me, my sis seemed more intrigued by fetishism than repulsed.

Slamming her precious bag of pretzels on the desk, she growled, "I can't believe he said those things about his own son, and I can't believe you're just up and leaving and continuing to work for that asshole. Damn—" She looked at the bag. "Now I'll have to eat the crumbs."

"Are you pregnant?" Sacrificing a bag of food seemed over the top, even for Melissa.

"What? No, just...low blood sugar. These are helping." She nibbled on a crumb. "You have to get in touch with him before you go."

"I've tried. Aside from sitting outside his apartment and acting like a stalker, which I'm definitely not going to do, I've done everything I can."

"Mm-hmm."

"Don't 'mm-hmm' me. That's like calling me a dumbass. I know that mm-hmm."

"Well…" she said in a singsong.

"Brat." I swiped the bag away from her and ate pretzel crumbs. They were delicious.

"So that's it then? You two are done?"

"I don't want to be. Cornering him at your clinic was my last resort." I unzipped the pocket of my satchel and pulled out a rectangular box with blue wrapping paper—my gift to Oisin. "Would you make sure he gets it? I intended to give it to him the night we fought and never got the chance."

"What is it?"

"A surprise."

"You're no fun." She put the envelope in the desk drawer with the letter from her advisor. "I'm sorry about you and Os. But I think he'll come around. Just give him some time."

"Thanks, Sis. I hope you're right."

The front door opened, and a bulldog and his owner waddled in.

"Hey, Jimmy," Melissa greeted her client.

"I'll let you get back to work."

"Dinner at Mom's this weekend? We'll have a little goodbye party."

"I'll be there."

I returned to work, trying not to let my mind drift to Oisin. I felt infected, like he'd gotten under my skin and injected himself into every cell of my being. It'd been the same since the first night we'd met. And all those cells told me he wanted me as much as I wanted him, which rendered me clueless as to why he'd stormed out on us and continued ignoring me.

I wasn't about to beg him or text him repeatedly. It was up to him to contact me. My gift, though it was never meant to be a parting gift, would ensure him a fresh start, one I'd originally hoped to share with him. Something the bullheaded man would've discovered if he'd heard me out. We'd be miles apart in a few weeks, and if amends weren't made between us, then everything that had happened in Vegas would stay in Vegas, just like the city's infamous slogan touted.

# Chapter Twenty-Two

OISIN

It'd been three long weeks since I'd volunteered at Paws for Love and I missed Melissa and the furries. So when she called saying her receptionist/vet tech had gone home sick and she needed some extra assistance with the troops, I went in. I'd been avoiding anything Trent related, including the man himself. The voicemail he'd left after we fought stayed on my cell phone. I listened to it more times than I cared to count, missing the sound of his voice.

I pushed open the door to find a full waiting room: two cats in carriers, three dogs of various sizes, a bunny, and the office cat, Maurice, who sat on the reception desk overlooking the patients. The clinic smelled of lavender cleaner and animal fur. Melissa had explained to me that the scent of certain disinfectants increased anxiety in the animals, and this one kept them as calm as possible. Judging by the whimpers of the shaking English spaniel and the ultra-relaxed French bulldog that lay on his belly with his back legs splayed outward, the serene odor effected only a portion of patients.

"Thank God you're here," Melissa said when she entered the reception area. Her hair spun out from her bun in unruly strands, looking like a Fourth of July sparkler, and she had puffy half-moons under her eyes and a pink nose that looked raw from blowing it too much. "Can you check the patients out? Mrs. Garcia and Mr. Thomas are ready to leave." Melissa took a tissue from her pocket and wiped her nose. "I'll try not to pass this on to you. It's a nasty spring cold. But just because I'm desperate for help and grateful you're here doesn't mean you get out of explaining why you've been 404 later, when it's not a madhouse."

I deserved that. "I'm sorry. I've had a lot to think about lately."

"I bet. Tell me later, okay?" Melissa went to the woman with the nervous spaniel and took the dog's leash. Before she went to the examination room, she stopped and said, "There are a few things on the desk I need you to look at after you've finished."

"No problem." I went over to the desk and typed in Mrs. Garcia's name on the computer. The screen became populated with her pet's information and the invoice for the nail trimming and vaccination shots for her cats, Lulu and Lety. The temperamental credit card machine had been updated to a modern one that worked flawlessly.

The first hour flew by as I got lost in the simple transactions, doing my best to forget about Trent and that this was his sister's clinic. Maurice occasionally bumped my hand, eager to be scratched on his neck. The orange tabby weighed around twenty pounds, fitting for his long length.

Melissa appeared from an exam room with the final patient of the evening. "Bring Elsa back next week and I'll remove the stitches." The white dog had a fierce underbite, complete with an incisor that sprang out sideways. I checked Elsa out and made the follow-up appointment.

"Thanks, Os." Melissa leaned against the door. I'd never seen her look so exhausted.

"Do you need help cleaning up?"

"No, that's okay. Jenny will be in early tomorrow to take care of it." She nudged her chin in the direction of the computer. "Did you look in the bag yet?"

I scanned the desk and found a white bag with the Paws for Love logo and my name on it sitting by the computer. "What is this?" I asked, picking it up.

She pushed herself off the wall and walked toward me. "Why don't you open it and find out?"

A letter and a long box with blue wrapping paper sat inside. I opened the letter and had to read it twice. "You got me work-study? Melissa!" I rushed up and hugged her, lifting and spinning her, not caring about catching her cold. "Thank you. This is amazing."

"The box isn't from me, and I have no idea what it is."

There was only one other person it might be from. My heart pumped fiercely, drowning out all sound as I peeled away the paper. The envelope inside had the UC Davis logo.

"No, he didn't do this. He couldn't have." I stared at the letter from the bursar's office. "I'm not reading this right. I can't be."

Melissa stood next to me and looked at the paper. "He did. Oh, brother." She shook her head. "Oisin, that man is head over heels for you. If you don't make amends, I'm gonna have to pull a big sister move and disown you." The playfulness in her voice belied her frustration. I had nothing to worry about...aside from Trent paying the entire first year of tuition.

"I can't accept this. There's no way." I put the paper back in the box along with the work-study approval letter. "You guys are... Thank you."

"I don't know what happened between the two of you that you don't want to talk to him, but get over it. He deserves better, Os."

"I'll go talk to him. I'll stop by the firm on the way home tonight."

"He won't be there."

"Why?"

"He moved back to Los Angeles a few days ago."

A rock dropped in my stomach. "Looks like I'm going to LA." I had some room on my credit card to buy a flight. But I had no idea if I wanted to apologize for being too scared to be with him, or to give back the money, or what exactly. I just knew I had to see him.

THE FLIGHT TOOK less time than it did to find Trent's West Hollywood condo, or at least it felt that way as my taxi crawled through the LA streets. I paid the driver and studied the unimpressive multistory unit. Tan walls held back the small trees and shrubs surrounding the entrance and a red awing hung over the stairwell leading to the doorway. Everything had a faint gray patina of smog.

I shuffled up the stairs to the set of glass doors and found the buzzer with Trent's last name beside it. My hand trembled as I hovered over the button. I'd had an entire plane ride to figure out what to say, and I still had no idea. A young woman exiting the building held the door open. I thanked her and slipped through, hoping something brilliant would come to me while I searched for Trent's condo.

A large atrium teeming with rosemary, white roses, and a few desert plants filled the center of the complex. Its beauty made the outside of the building seem like a front, a protective clamshell to hide the pearl inside. It was nice. Peaceful. I wasn't. Sweat beaded across my brow, and my shirt stuck to my back. The hot weather was partly to blame.

I reached Trent's door and hesitated a fraction too long. The door swung open, and Trent's face went through a metamorphosis of emotion from wide-eyed surprise, to a partial smile showing off those teeth I loved, and then a quick mask, as if he remembered he was mad.

"You're the last person I expected." He leaned against the doorframe, sweaty, blocking me from entering. I'd interrupted his workout, judging by the track pants and silky workout shirt he was wearing. I wanted to get up all in that—wrap myself around him like a spider monkey and lick the sweat off him.

"I can come back if I disturbed you." *Please let me inside.*

He shook his head. "Oh, Os." The anger dissolved, and he gestured for me to come in. Stepping into his condo was like seeing a new side of my lover. If he was still my lover. Pictures of his family, especially his niece, lined the hallway leading to the open living room. The streamlined décor suited him. Modern. Sleek. The furnishings were black-and-white, and his living room had a large carpet with a geometric print covering the hardwood floor.

I followed him into the kitchen, where he grabbed a half-full sport drink off the counter and took a sip. He put it down and combed his fingers through his hair. "You never called."

"I was upset." I fidgeted with my fingers. "I-I didn't want to—"

In two strides, Trent came to me and hugged me, rubbing his hands along my back. "You should've called." The softness of his beard grazed my cheek. We exchanged desperate, hungry kisses. He stole my breath, my thoughts, and my worries as my body yielded to every brush of his tongue, spiking the urgent need to feel all of him buried inside me. I'd been an idiot, trying to run away from this. Trent was worth the risk, worth giving up—or at least postponing—my aspirations.

"Need you," he breathed between our kisses. He lifted my shirt, and I pulled it over my head, grateful to remove the sweaty thing and more than grateful to have Trent's tongue licking and teeth biting my nipples. Step by slow step, he walked us into the living room and pushed me to the edge of the sofa, where he popped open the button on my pants and forced them down to my ankles. Without hesitating, he turned me around and folded me in half over the arm, ass high and in full view.

"Beautiful." He groaned as he spread my cheeks, wetting my hole with his fingers. "This is mine, Os. You're mine," he rasped, anger and lust thickened his voice.

Yes, I was his. I'd been his since our first night together. He'd spoiled me for any other lover.

I heard the rustle of fabric, and soon his length slid between my cheeks and pushed under my balls. "Trent," I whimpered, wanting him inside me and fucking me senseless. "Please."

"Please what?" He smacked my ass cheek. The abrupt pain rocketed to my dick, turning it solid. He knew spanking got me harder than a two-by-four.

"Please fuck me, Sir," I pleaded, knowing how much he loved it when I asked. I pushed my ass back toward him. I was so fucking hungry for his cock.

"Put your hands on the sofa and keep them there." Latching onto to my hips, he forced me to take several backward steps until my torso was parallel with the floor. He tugged off my shoes and one of my pant's legs, leaving the other bunched around my ankle. "Stay just like that." Soft steps padded away.

I waited, not moving, letting seconds pass by. Seconds turned to what felt like minutes, and I wondered what game Trent was up to. Humiliation crept over me. Was this a test? Was he messing with me? I deserved it. I'd been the one who walked out on him at the restaurant, the one who'd decided I couldn't be with him.

"Trent?" I called, still standing, ass exposed. There was movement from another room followed by the sound of his footsteps approaching. I could feel his eyes on me. I pushed off the sofa and turned to face him, noticing a leather paddle in one of his hands and supplies in the other.

"No, you just want me now. You walked away from me, Os." Abruptly, he shoved me back in position with unexpected force. "Don't move. Not yet." He smacked the other ass cheek, causing my cock to leak. *Why the hell was that so hot?* "Tell me why you're here."

"I-I came to apologize." There was the snick of a bottle being opened and he slicked cool gel between my ass cheeks, breaching me with his long fingers. I pushed back, welcoming the intrusion, but a strong hand grabbed my hip preventing me from moving. He removed his fingers.

"Don't stop!" I whimpered.

"Face forward, Oisin," he growled. "You think you deserve this?" He batted his dick against my ass. "You left me at the restaurant and wouldn't return my phone calls."

"I know. I'm sorry, it was—"

Trent nudged the tip of his dick into my entrance and pushed, taking away any coherent thought I had.

"You feel so good." I rested my forehead on the top of the sofa. All my focus was on the dick impaling me, stretching and burning as Trent and I became one.

Twining his fingers with mine, he whispered in my ear, taking on a far sweeter tone than the angry Dom. "I've missed you, Os."

"I've missed you, too. I'm so sorry."

He brushed his lips along that sensitive area on my neck, the one that sent tingles to my belly. "You drive me crazy." Goose bumps trailed along my back chasing his fingertips. "I was so mad at you for being such a brat, for shutting me out of your life after I told you I loved you."

He rocked his hips, dragging his thick cock back and forth in long, slow thrusts. I hated it and loved it. I needed him to move faster, to fuck me into oblivion, to hit that spot inside that made my dick weep for him.

"I should punish you."

*Fuck, that's hot.*

I swallowed as my dick dripped. "H-How?"

"Do you want me to punish you?" he asked, and I turned my head and saw a mischievous sparkle in his blue eyes.

"Um, yes? I mean, I guess I deserve it. I was kinda a brat, like you said."

He laughed. "Does this mean you consent to whatever punishment I give you?"

"Will I like it?" If it had something to do with that paddle he brought out, I already knew I'd like it.

"It's punishment. The idea isn't for you to like it, but *I* will."

"Okay."

"*Okay?* Say, 'Yes, Sir.'"

I stifled a nervous chuckle. "Yes, Sir."

"Good boy." He withdrew from me, pulled off his shirt, and tied the fabric over my eyes so I couldn't see anything. "Keep your hands there and spread your legs wider... Beautiful." The palm of his hand smoothed over the flesh of my ass. "Ten hits, five on each side. I'll start off light and get harder. You will count each one out loud. Understand?"

"Yes, Sir." I tensed, bracing for the pain to come.

*Smack!*

"One."

*Smack!*

"Two." Three and four and five got harder, like he'd warned. By six and seven, the pain caused sweat to bead across my forehead and all my muscle tensed. But my dick? That thing begged for release.

"Eight! Oh! Fuck! That *hurt!*" Searing pain, hot as an iron, branded my ass, sending me onto my toes.

"It's supposed to. It's punishment, remember?"

"Nine! Ouch, fuck! Ten!"

"Good boy." Trent slid his warm hand around my stiff cock, pumping me. "Now you can get your reward."

"You inside me?"

"Are you sure you can take me slamming up against your pretty pink ass?"

"No, but it's been too long." I stood up and removed the blindfold.

He paused, searching my face for something before placing a soft kiss on my lips. The contrast from the pain he'd inflicted moments ago had my head spinning. "Turn around, babe and spread out just like before."

Without hesitation, he buried his cock inside of me, and started fucking, pegging that spot that made me lose all sense of self. My world narrowed down to where we were connected. This moment needed to last forever. Too bad it wouldn't. I squeezed around Trent's cock as I teetered on the edge.

"Come for me, babe." All it took was the brush of his fingers along my shaft to send me flying. Stars, moons, galaxies flashed before me as I pulsed until I nearly blacked out. He yelled, the cry distant in my orgasmic state as his hot come filled the condom.

He collapsed on my back, holding me, his heartbeat pounding as he caught his breath. "This doesn't mean I forgive you." Tender kisses on my neck and light caresses along my stomach and chest had me convinced otherwise.

"But does it mean you'll let me touch you?" I ached to do so.

Warm hands guided me upright, gently turning me so I faced him. Blood rushed back into my arms. A trail of hot come dribbled down my inner thigh, audibly hitting the wood floor.

"So fucking hot." Trent reached between my legs and scooped it with his fingers. He licked it and pressed his fingers to my mouth, feeding me the remainder. The last bits of self-preservation untwined, leaving me one thin thread away from forgetting about Davis, forgetting about the world beyond this room as I rested in his muscular arms.

"I'm sorry. I was afraid…" The air grew impossibly heavy as I uttered my confession. "I was afraid if I stayed with you, I'd never leave Vegas, that I'd never go to Davis, and I'd done that before. But when Melissa gave me your gift—I can't believe you paid for my tuition—I had to see you, and I got on the earliest flight I could." I inhaled his scent at the juncture of his neck and shoulder and placed a tender kiss there. The smell of sweat and sex clung to him, and dang, it was sexy.

"I never asked you to choose," he crooned. "I would never do that, Os."

"Then how did you see us working out? How could we be together if you were in Vegas and I was in California? Did you think my dad wouldn't care?"

"I've been questioning a lot of things in my life, prioritizing." He picked up a small bottle from the floor and squirted the lotion in his hand and rubbed my sore cheeks. The second the cool gel touched my ass, the fire went out.

I groaned with relief. "That's so much better."

"Don't want that pretty skin to hurt too long." He pulled up his track pants and went into the adjoining kitchen and got a towel. Squatting, he wiped the come off my leg and the floor and noticed the stain I'd left on the back of his sofa.

"Um, yeah. Had no control over that, sorry." I stepped back into my pants and zipped up.

"I think it's an improvement." Funny how something so ridiculous could trigger a swarm of butterflies. He complimented my come and I got butterflies. WTF? Running a hand through his hair, he puffed out a breath. "We should sit." We rounded the sofa, leaving behind my christening, and sat. A large flat-panel TV hung on the wall across from us, a gas fireplace to the right. It was a cozy little room. I briefly wondered how many nights he and Nic had spent cuddled on this sofa watching television or screwing while the fireplace blazed in the background.

"I told your father about us."

The earth dropped out from under me. "Why? He fired you, didn't he? Oh my God, that's really why you're in LA. He denied you the promotion and made you so uncomfortable that you wanted to quit. Trent, this was exactly why I didn't want you to say anything. You're getting screwed out of the partnership you worked your butt off for." For the first time in over a month, I itched to call my father so I could tell him what a piece of trash he was. He had no morals when it came to his family or his loyal employees. Or was it ethics? Either way, he sucked.

"Can I ask you something? Do you know who Kyle Hernandez is?"

An icy mixture of rage and insecurity ripped through me. That had been one of my worst and most humiliating experiences. I'd been on my knees, listening to Kyle praise me about how skilled my mouth was one minute and the next feeling his boot in my stomach, kicking me after I'd swallowed his come. I'd staggered into my father's office hours after going to urgent care to make sure nothing was broken, only to find the hot lawyer I'd been with weeks before had been assigned as my babysitter.

I bit my lip. "He graduated last semester. How do you know Kyle, and what does that have to do with you telling my father about us?" Saying his name made me feel sick.

"Before I left, I interviewed him for a clerk position, and he mentioned you. Did you date him?"

"What?" I almost vomited the peanuts I'd eaten on the plane ride. "No, I...I sucked him off at a club, and then he kicked the shit out of me. Why are we talking about him?"

"He did what? Why didn't you press charges?"

"It'd create too much drama. His parents are district attorneys, and my dad, being who his is—it'd be a mess. Besides, it'd be my word against his, and you know that doesn't hold up in court." Kyle deserved punishment but I had little faith justice would be served. He'd get a smack on the wrist and possibly do some community service, if he got any sentencing at all. Maybe it was cowardly of me not to press charges, but I wanted to put it behind me.

Trent beckoned me to sit closer and put his arm around me. I snuggled into him, finding the perfect spot. "The kid is an arrogant prick, something your dad and I agreed on. Drama or not, you should press charges. You might not be the only one he's hurt."

"I'm not going to do that, Trent. Drop it, okay?"

"Okay," he relented. "For now."

"What does Kyle have to do with any of this anyway?"

"Kyle said he saw us at the pizza place together and threatened to tell your father about us."

I squirmed, suddenly uncomfortable. "You could've denied there was anything going on between us. Dad would've thought you were mentoring me, just like we'd planned to say if we ever got caught by one of your coworkers." Fighting was exhausting. Or maybe it was the postorgasmic tiredness setting in. There was no energy left for me be angry with him over Kyle.

"I could've, you're right." He wound his arm tighter, pressing me into his chest. "When I first joined the firm, Harrison was my mentor, someone I respected, admired, and modeled my work ethic after. Working the way I did afforded me things. A nice home. A nice car. All the fancy amenities a cushy job and a Hollywood home allowed, without any time to enjoy them. That was okay for a while. I believed the promotion was everything I wanted—until I met you. Then, having things mattered less."

Absentmindedly, he ran his fingers through my hair, soothing me. I wanted to stay like this, to be with him, but I couldn't ask him to move to Davis with me. Could I?

"My opinion of your father changed after I moved to Vegas. He lied to you and to your mother, and I refuse to be like him in that way. I disliked sneaking around town, not being able to be proud to be with you. It was suffocating, like living in the closet. I don't see how loving you could be wrong, Oisin, and hiding it is too painful." He skimmed his fingers along my cheek, delicate and tender. "I don't want to be that person with secrets, surrounded by all these beautiful things while my personal life falls apart. I've been through that once already. The choice between having you in my life or a job that offers a whole lot of emptiness is an easy one."

I slipped through his arms and straddled him, excitement tingling along my limbs...*all* my limbs. "What are you saying?"

"I'm saying I want to be with you, that all this—" He waved his hand, motioning to the room around us. "It doesn't matter. You do."

"Did you...were you going to come with me to Davis?" I searched his ocean eyes and saw love reflecting back.

"Yes, depending on if I could find work there or San Francisco. Your dream is important to me. Seeing you happy is important to me. Once your father severed your trust fund, I knew financial help from your parents wouldn't be an option, and you'd miss the enrollment date for next semester. Your tuition is paid for. You can pay me back if you want, once you graduate."

I stared at him, overwhelmed by a tsunami of love and lust for this incredible man who'd left me speechless. "I-I don't know what to say."

"You're not going to storm off like a brat this time?" he teased.

"No. I'm sorry about that. I should've talked with you and not freaked out. Can I make it up to you?"

"You'd better." He devoured my lips, and we were gone on each other the rest of the day and night as I made amends.

# Chapter Twenty-Three

OISIN

The past few months had gone by in a blur, and I was leaving for California in a couple of hours. I'd signed up for a class during the summer session and hoped to find some part-time work before the fall semester started. This was the last time I'd wake up in my childhood home, and it wasn't because I was moving. As part of the divorce settlement, Mom and Dad were selling the house. Lying in bed, I watched as the sun rose, casting a pink-orange glow into the bedroom. As a kid, I hadn't appreciated my home. Having lived in an apartment smaller than this bedroom had changed my perspective. I'd had a good childhood. I was fortunate.

After I got ready, Devon came over and joined my mom and me for breakfast, and then the two of us retreated to my bedroom, along with Maggie, to finish packing.

"I can't believe you're really leaving." Devon plopped down on my bed and Maggie curled up on the floor beside him.

"I can't believe you're wearing all green. You look like a giant leprechaun."

"Monochrome is the latest trend." Devon rested a hand on his hip. "You, sir, lack the proper respect for the fashion industry." Typical BFF banter. "You'll see, once you get out amongst all those Californian hotties."

"I'm sure." I began filling the suitcase with the remaining items. I'd packed most of it the night before and earlier that day before Devon arrived.

"Do you like your new apartment?"

"The pictures Trent sent look good. He said it's nice, clean, and there's a small yard for Maggie." Hearing her name mentioned, Maggie wagged her tail. Trent had interviews in the San Francisco area last month and took a side trip to find an apartment in Davis for Maggie and me. He'd even offered to pay the deposit. I declined.

I disliked that Trent had paid for my tuition, and I intended to pay him back with interest. I forced him to draw up a contract stating that as well. Having my father hold my trust over me was one thing. Knowing I owed my boyfriend a substantial amount of money left our relationship out of balance, and the sooner I could reimburse him, the better I'd feel.

I zipped and locked my suitcase and sat beside Devon. "How's it going with Stone?"

My friend's dimpled smile appeared. "Good. Actually, better than good. I can't believe we've been living together two months already." He glowed with happiness. "He'll have to leave at the end of the month for a tour, but I'm joining him for a few weeks in July." He lay down, resting his head on my thighs, and looked up at me. "I'm gonna miss you, Os."

I twirled a lock of his sandy-brown hair. "I'll come back to see you." I meant it. I'd miss him, my brother, and my mother too much to stay away.

"You'd better. At least come back for the holidays. I don't know how I'd survive a Harrison Family Thanksgiving or Christmas without you."

"Dev, that's months away. And of course I'm coming back for the holidays. Trent's family is here as well."

"You know what I'm saying." He rolled his eyes.

I did. Goodbyes were hard.

With a sigh, Devon stood. "Charlie's got this custom truck coming in, so I gotta go home and change. No sense in ruining my stunning leprechaun ensemble." He took my hands and pulled me off the bed and into his arms, squeezing the air from me. "I love you, Os."

"I love you, too."

"Good thing I didn't wear makeup today." He sniffled and wiped his eyes. "Come on. Let's load up your car." After popping the handle on the suitcase, Devon wheeled it behind him as he left my bedroom.

"You ready, Maggie?" Big brown eyes seemed to smile at me, and her tail thwacked the bed as she wagged. "Let's go." I took one final look at my old bedroom and crossed the threshold, ready to pursue my new life.

"Do you have everything you need?" Mom asked as we walked down the hallway to the front door.

"Yeah, I'm all set. I even have Maggie's food and water bowl. Dev made sure the car was in top shape, too."

Devon nodded in confirmation.

As I exited with my suitcase in tow, an unexpected visitor showed up. Just the sight of him had me tingling with happiness. I launched into Trent's arms, attacking him with a kiss that might have been a little too R-rated for the surrounding company.

"Miss me much?" he asked, breathless.

"Nah."

"Brat." Trent pinched my waist, causing me to yelp and swat him off.

"Quit it!" I tried to get him back, but he moved too quickly.

He scooped me into his arms, rubbing his nose against mine. "You love it."

Maybe not "it," but I did love him, and if my family wasn't watching I'd have nibbled on his earlobe and told him all the dirty things I'd like to do to him to prove how much I did.

Maggie barked at us in protest. "Someone's jealous," Trent said and set me down. "Never thought I'd have to compete with a hairy lady for my boyfriend's attention."

"There's no competition." I nuzzled against his neck and planted a kiss there.

My mother came toward us, saying, "Don't hog my future son-in-law. C'mere, Trent, and give me a hug."

I think I turned about forty shades of red. "Mom," I scolded. "Don't scare him away."

"Have you seen the way this man looks at you? I don't think it's possible to scare him away."

"It'd take a lot more than the threat of tying the knot with you to scare me away." Trent winked at me and gave my mom a hug. The innuendo shot straight to my dick. He'd tied me up and used some of his fun toys on me the last time we'd had sex. Hotter than hell. Even better when we switched it up.

"Good to see you again," Devon said and hugged Trent once Mom was done. Seeing my best friend and my boyfriend get along so well made me a little teary. It affirmed how perfectly Trent fit into my life, how accepting he was of my family, even after the way my father had treated him. He cared not only about me, but the people who were important to me.

"Oisin didn't tell me you were joining him." Mom seemed relieved I wouldn't be making the drive solo. I would have enjoyed the alone time, but sharing the journey with Trent would make it better. Maybe even test our relationship out by being crammed together for hours. It'd definitely test my ability to keep my hands off him while driving. As fun as the last seventy-five mile-per-hour blow job was, it wasn't worth risking our lives, or Maggie's.

"Since I don't start my new job until next week, I thought I'd surprise him." He grinned.

"You flew all the way from San Francisco to turn around and drive eight hours with my son? That's so sweet." Mom wiped the corners of her eyes, trying to hide her tears. "I'm sorry." She sniffled. "I always hoped my son would fall in love with someone who cared about him as deeply as you do, Trent."

He rubbed the back of his neck, uncomfortable and cute as hell. "He's worth it." That sheepish lovestruck gaze in his eyes was tempting me to grab him and run up to my bedroom to show him precisely how valuable I could be.

"You're so grown up now, Os. Going out of state for school. Falling in love with probably the only decent attorney out there." Mom had every right to be jaded after what Dad had put her through. "I'm happy for you both." She wiped her face again. "Enough of that. Let's get you packed and ready to go."

We crammed the last of my luggage into the car next to several boxes of essentials I had left over from my student apartment. It'd be tight, but the three of us would fit.

"I'm so proud of you, honey," Mom croaked, wiping a stray hair from my eyes. "Once the divorce is settled, I'll be able to cover your tuition." Mom had gone to her attorney when I'd told her about the freeze on my trust, like she promised. But the attorney had said there wasn't anything she could do, that the way the trust was set up, either parent could shut me out of it without the other's consent. I'd never heard her swear so much about something than when she heard that news.

"I've got to get to work, guys," Devon said. He hugged my mom goodbye and then scooped me up in an embrace. "I'll see you soon."

"You will." Leaving Devon behind caused a bittersweet ache in my chest. I'd miss us living in the same city, miss being able to razz him about his outfits, miss our Girls Night Out.

Trent pulled me in close and wrapped his arm over my shoulders. We watched Devon get into his classic Chevy and drive down the long driveway just as a familiar Mercedes drove up.

"Well, there goes the neighborhood," my mother grumbled.

I couldn't agree more. As tempting as it was, it'd be immature to jump in the car and drive off before my father could speak to me.

He got out of his car, a briefcase in one hand and an unreadable expression on his face, and approached. He'd aged these past few months. Gray hair spread beyond his temples, and the lines in his face had deepened. He looked tired, too. If he'd shown any remorse or apologized for hurting Mom, Trent, or me, I might feel bad for him.

"Angel."

Mom squared her shoulders and stood taller. "Andrew."

Ignoring the cold greeting, my father directed his attention to Trent and me. "Mr. Fisher."

"Mr. Harrison." Definitely no love lost between them.

"Oisin, I spoke to your brother, and he said you were leaving today. I'm glad I caught you before you did."

I folded my arms across my chest. "Why? Did you want to get in one last dig before I left?"

My dad's stoic facade softened. "I remember when you were born. It was two and half weeks past the due date. Your mother and I joked about how you were going to be a stubborn child. And now look at you. Moving on to become a veterinarian."

"No thanks to you." Okay, so I was being juvenile. Maybe I hadn't grown up as much as I'd thought.

"I only wanted what was best for you, son."

"No, Dad, you didn't. You wanted me to be like you, to take over the company. And then you got mad when I changed my mind. You did the same thing to Dan."

"Your brother has complete control of his trust. He's had it since he graduated two years ago. And I got mad because you were failing and not acting like yourself. I got mad because you were upsetting your mother. It had nothing to do with me expecting you to work at the firm. Had you come to me and told me about your plans to go into veterinary medicine earlier, I'd have..."

He pinched the bridge of his nose. "I didn't come here to fight. I came here to give you this." He tossed his briefcase on the hood of my car, opened it, and handed me papers clipped together with a check on the top. "I modified your trust. The amount will be deposited automatically into your account monthly just as before. The check will cover the moneys you owe Mr. Fisher. When the next semester's tuition is due, you'll be able to pay for it and any supplies directly from your trust."

I stared at the papers in disbelief. My father had changed the terms to what they were when I'd started law school. The check amount covered the year's tuition. There had to be a catch. "What changed your mind?"

"First, it is important you do well, Oisin, and I'd rather not have you struggle financially while attending grad school. You're too smart to waste your time with some menial job that barely pays for basic living expenses." He looked at Trent, and the coldness in his eyes told me whatever he had to say next was going to be unpleasant. "Second, I'm concerned about your arrangement with Mr. Fisher. There were rumors, son. Things about him and his former lover that have me questioning your safety and the effects on your mental health." He kept his glacial stare fixed on my boyfriend. "I'd rather you not be indebted to him."

"That's bullshit, Harrison," Trent snarled as he took a step toward my father. "You have no right to bring that up."

I put my hand on Trent's chest, holding him back, and looked at my father. "What are you talking about?"

Dad rocked on his heels. "I'm talking about a deviant lifestyle."

I burst out into laughter. Deviant? Being a Dom was his past. And even if it wasn't, I never thought of BDSM as deviant.

"Oisin, what is your father talking about?" Mom asked.

"Something that is none of his business." I tossed my hands up. "Dad keeps thinking he has to control me. That I'm incapable of making decisions about my life, and then he interferes when I actually do."

"If you didn't keep making insane decisions, I wouldn't have to interfere. Trenton Fisher is an excellent attorney, but not someone I want with my son."

I bristled, shaking while I spoke. "First, what I do with my boyfriend is none of your freaking business, and second, at least he's never cheated on me or lied to me like you did to Mom." Yeah, I took the dig and tossed his words and actions back at him. If my dad thought butting into my sex life was okay, then I had every right to bring up his infidelity. "Did you give me my trust fund back as a bribe to keep me away from Trent? If that's why, then I don't want it. My heart is with Trent. I'm not leaving him." I took Trent's hand in mine.

My father plastered on his game face. "If you can't care enough for your own mental health to see the detrimental effects of being with that man, then there's nothing more I can do. Keep the trust. At least I'll know you won't have to be dependent on Fisher." He took another document out of his briefcase before closing and removing it from the car.

As upset as I was about what my father had said and done, I didn't want my last memory of us to be a fight. I'd already spent the last few months being mad at him, and I hated it.

"Trust me, Dad. For once, I actually know what I'm doing."

He shifted his gaze from Trent to me and said, "I hope so." Holding out the papers he'd pulled from his briefcase, he directed his attention to my mother. "Angel. Despite what my attorneys have advised, here is the deed to the house. It's all yours to do with as you like."

Her jaw clenched as she accepted them.

"It doesn't make up for what I did, and I am sorry I hurt you and our family."

At last, the man showed some remorse. I think I finally understood how you could love someone and not like them.

Mom stood a little taller. "You're right. It doesn't make up for it. Now, please leave. I'd like to speak with Oisin before he has to go."

Dad pursed his lips and looked down. The expression was as close to dejection as I'd ever seen on him. "Have a safe trip, Os." Looking resigned, he returned to his car and left.

Mom hugged me. "I'm glad he finally reinstated your trust, honey. You're going to be fine out there."

"And you will, too. You don't have to move." Mom loved that house and all the memories of us growing up in it. I hated the thought of her being forced out of it.

"Will you two be back for Thanksgiving?" she asked. "If so, you're both welcome to stay here. There's plenty of room."

I looked at Trent. "Yes," he replied. "We'll be here. Though my mom might put up a fight over whose house we stay at."

Leaning into my boyfriend, I whispered, "We can't have kinky sex at either of our parents' houses. I opt for a hotel room."

"Oisin Harrison, I'm going to pretend I didn't hear that!" Mom laughed as she covered her ears.

After more hugs and a few tears, Maggie, Trent, and I piled into my car and waved goodbye to Mom.

"Thank you," Trent said and kissed the back of my hand.

"What for?" I risked a glance at him as I drove.

"Standing up to your father like that. Defending us. I know how difficult that was for you to do."

"I told you, I'm done with my dad and everyone else telling me what is and isn't good for me. I love you, and he should respect my decision. No one has the right to judge you or me for the way we have sex. That's ridiculous. We're not doing anything wrong, and when you were with Nic, you weren't either." After our last little sex adventure, I was certain Trent knew I didn't share my father's distorted view of BDSM, but I wanted to assure him just the same.

"You're incredibly sexy when you're all fired up. I like this side of you."

"It's gonna be a long trip if you keep purring in my ear like that."

"Delayed gratification makes things so much better, don't you agree?"

I groaned. Already, there was less room in my pants. "You're worth the wait."

"So are you."

WHEN WE CROSSED the state line into California, a sense of achievement came over me. I'd finally found the courage to change my life, to take the wheel and go where I dreamed of for so long, thanks to the wonderful man beside me. I reached over and touched Trent's arm. "I couldn't have done this without you. Thank you."

"I can't take all the credit." He moved his hand to the nape of my neck and started playing with the hair there. The light brush of his fingertips in such a sensitive area had me wanting to curl up in his lap and let him pet me like a cat.

*Focus and drive!*

"What do you mean?"

"It seems to me your parents would've supported you no matter what career you'd chosen. Your dad, for all his flaws, gave you the financial support to follow your dream. And your mom, she definitely has your back. What changed was you, Os. You let me help you. You trusted me enough to accept my love and support, and you decided what I offered was the best thing for you."

"Trenton Fisher, you're a good man, and if I weren't driving right now, I'd be straddling you and ravaging that beautiful mouth of yours."

"If you weren't driving right now, we'd be having crazy monkey sex."

"Bakersfield is about halfway to Davis. I say we spend the night."

"I say that's a perfect idea."

# Epilogue

OISIN

The summer session at UC Davis had just ended, and Maggie and I left immediately for San Francisco to see Trent. We'd spent the summer meeting halfway between Davis and San Francisco on the weekends, both of us making the best of the short amount of time we had as his new job and my studies fought for our attention. During our weekends together we learned about each other, dated, and explored our sexual dynamics. I'd worn the kilt several times. There was nothing like a nice breeze to stave off the heat. He'd introduced me to a little bit of bondage and edging, which was about the hottest freaking thing I'd ever experienced. I happily reciprocated the treatment and Trent had been more than appreciative. I'd kept my cross-dressing limited to fun underwear until Devon visited last month. He had the makeup magic to make me pretty, and we'd done a Girls Night Out with our boyfriends. Life couldn't be better, not really.

Trent had recently moved into a townhouse close to his new firm and within walking distance to the beach. When I arrived, he gave us the tour. Built sometime in the 20s or 30s, though recently updated, the house had vintage charm enhanced by the addition of a modern stove and dishwasher, key essentials in my opinion. There was a dire need for furniture. Trent had two chairs, a table, his bed, a nightstand, and a couple lamps.

"This is ours, Oisin," he said between kisses so soft and sweet they melted me. "I realize this might be too fast, but I'd like you to move in. I want to see your gorgeous body next to me in our bed." He slid his hands along my back before resting them along my waist. "I want your belongings here, reminding me of you, of us, while you're away at school. I want you to call this home with me."

"With the way you're kissing me, there's no way I could refuse." I'd been thinking the same thing anyway, though something more legally binding. I couldn't help it; I was the marrying kind.

Trent pushed me against the bedroom wall, continuing our kisses. He pulled my shirt over my head only to stop before completely removing it, leaving my wrists trapped in the material. Pausing, he waited for my go-ahead as lust poured from his stunning eyes.

"Don't stop." I needed to be naked and owned by this man.

"Keep your hands there." He leaned in, granting me a few more kisses as he unbuttoned my pants. With reverence, he lowered them, taking a painstaking amount of time. "I love these panties, so frilly." He snapped the band on the purple thong. I'd chosen them knowing he appreciated my underwear kink as much as I loved wearing silky things. But right now, I needed nakedness.

"You're killing me!" I'd waited an entire week to be with him and had no patience. Looking down at him, I ordered, "Get them off already!"

He laughed and shot me a wicked smile, revealing those sexy teeth. "I'm going to make sure every inch of your body is given the attention it deserves. Every—" He kissed my left inner thigh. "—inch." He kissed my right inner thigh. The featherlight touch tingled and tickled. He settled on taunting my all-too-sensitive groin area, never once touching my balls or my dick, which were still encased in the cute panties. And I needed for him to touch me. *God, did I need him to touch me.*

"Please, Trent."

"On the bed," he whispered into my ear.

Finally! I shuffled over to the California king-size bed—grateful it was only a few steps away because walking kinda sucked with my pants limiting my movement—and sat.

Chuckling, Trent knelt and pulled off my pants.

"Sure, now you do that after making me walk."

"What fun is it if I don't make you work for it?" He threw the pants aside and removed his shirt, treating me to an eyeful of that beautiful torso. He'd been working out all summer and as a result his muscles were more defined than when we'd first met. If my hands had been free, I'd have been rubbing them all over those biceps and that chest.

"You like?" he said as he playfully posed with his arms flexed in a horseshoe shape like a bodybuilder. A four pack lined his abdomen.

"Oh yeah, I like."

He continued the show by peeling off his socks and swinging them like ropes at his hips a few times before flicking them across the room. Turning his back, he peeked over his shoulder as he slid out of his pants. No underwear. He wore only mischief as he shook his ass. He did a pathetic little dance—great attorney, horrible dancer—back toward me.

I bent down and nipped a ripe butt cheek.

"Ouch! You naughty boy!" He spun around, revealing his gorgeous, hard cock.

"Well then," I said as I ogled him. "You'd better punish me."

Continuing to torment me, he grazed his fingertips along my arms and down past my chest. He nipped at my earlobes—*groan*—just as his hand slid inside my underwear to lazily jack me, as if he had all the freaking time in the world. I suppose he did. His stroking kept me hard yet gave nothing that would ease this craving.

"Careful what you ask for, boy." His gravelly tone had me leaking.

Trent pushed me flat on my back, straddled my chest, and lined his erect dick inches away from my lips.

"I know exactly what I'm asking for." I licked the head, encouraging Trent. He tasted like salt and the new sandalwood soap he was using.

"Open up." Tentatively, Trent lowered himself into my mouth, letting me adjust to his width and length before pushing in completely.

I stayed focused on him, watching as his eyes grew hazy the deeper he went. As he slid himself in and out, I kept my mouth wide and my tongue flat and firm against the underside of his veiny cock, feeling the ridges as he moved. I lost all form when he quickened the pace, and spit slobbered down my chin as the salty taste of his arousal coated my tongue.

"So close," he groaned. "You feel so good." He gave a few more thrusts, slowing before withdrawing. "I want to come inside you, but not like this." He caressed my cheek with his thumb.

"Are you a mind reader? Because that's exactly what I was thinking."

"No, I'm just a horny boyfriend."

"Well, horny boyfriend—" I lifted my arms up to let him know I didn't want to be restrained, and without hesitating, he removed my shirt and tossed it on the floor. "—I hope you have that good kind of lube we used last time."

"You're such a spoiled brat." Before I knew what was happening, he turned me on my side and smacked my bottom, which I'm sure left a handprint behind. Pain shot right to my dick, like it always did, and made me so freaking hard.

"Hey!" I narrowed my eyes, feigning anger. "Mind the goods!"

"Oh, I'll mind them." Trent gently planted himself between my legs, forcing me on my back. "And lick them..." Wetness engulfed my nipple as he mouthed and suckled it. "And bite them..." He blew on one of the buds, and then took it between his teeth and bore down harder and harder.

"Fuck! Ouch!" It hurt like hell, but in that good way. "The other one is getting jealous." I threaded my fingers in his brown hair and guided him to the neglected nub where he repeated the blowing and biting. My cock responded, twitching between us. Damn, I loved that thrill of pain. We'd have to invest in nipple clamps.

I'm not sure when he got the lube from the nightstand—and it was the expensive kind I liked—but as he continued using his mouth to play with my nipples, he breached me with his fingers. I was a man in heaven. Trent knew just how to massage me. He toyed with my P-spot, keeping me right on the edge, seeking the next brush of his fingers and eager for his thick length to take over.

"Need...you...please..." The massage had my body tingling and toes curling.

He removed his fingers and grabbed a condom. After sliding it down his thick member, he added some lube and gave himself a few strokes when he caught me watching him. "Like what you see?" That monster was standing tall and ready to go. *Drool.*

"Very much." I had to touch him—had to give him a few pumps before he swatted my hand away.

He spread my legs and propped himself on one hand while guiding his length toward my entrance with the other. "You ready, babe?"

"Oh, hell yeah." I tightened my legs around his waist, feeling the tip breach me. Slowly, I pulled him inside.

Trent made love to me. Nothing rushed, just a slow steady rhythm. He had a knack for finding my sweet spot. Each push went deep enough to touch it, blending the pleasure-filled burn of him spreading me with that thick cock with another powerful sensation, one I couldn't pinpoint, yet heightened every nerve in my body. Need soon replaced tenderness, and Trent drove into me with intensity, staking his claim with every thrust until electricity tore up my spine, breaking me into a million pieces of orgasmic bliss.

"Focus on me." He took my head in his hands, and I dove into his ocean-colored eyes, watching them go hazy as a tangible supernova of energy erupted. "Fuck, Oisin!" His eyes rolled back, and his jaw went slack as his orgasm crashed down, dragging me along in his cosmic undertow.

"I love you," I whispered as I clung to him.

"I love you, too."

Quiet except for the sound of our breathing, we lay sated in each other's arms.

I had an amazing lover, a new home, a sweet dog, and was working toward a new career. It was too far to commute to Davis, and the next three years of seeing each other only on weekends or vacations were going to be difficult. We'd make it, though. For the first time in a long time, I had faith that love would last.

# About the Author

Grace Kilian Delaney resides in flammable Southern California where she spends the wee hours of the morning drinking coffee and writing. She identifies as genderfluid and bisexual, and a goal of hers is to create stories that include gay, bisexual, and genderfluid characters. When not writing, Grace composes music, pretends she's an opera singer, plays piano, and practices yoga, though not all at the same time.

Email: gracekiliandelaney@gmail.com

Facebook: www.facebook.com/GraceKilianD

Twitter: @GraceKilianD

Website: www.Gracekiliandelaney.wordpress.com

# Also Available from NineStar Press

# Connect with NineStar Press

www.ninestarpress.com

www.facebook.com/ninestarpress

www.facebook.com/groups/NineStarNiche

www.twitter.com/ninestarpress

www.tumblr.com/blog/ninestarpress